THE TRAITOR QUEEN

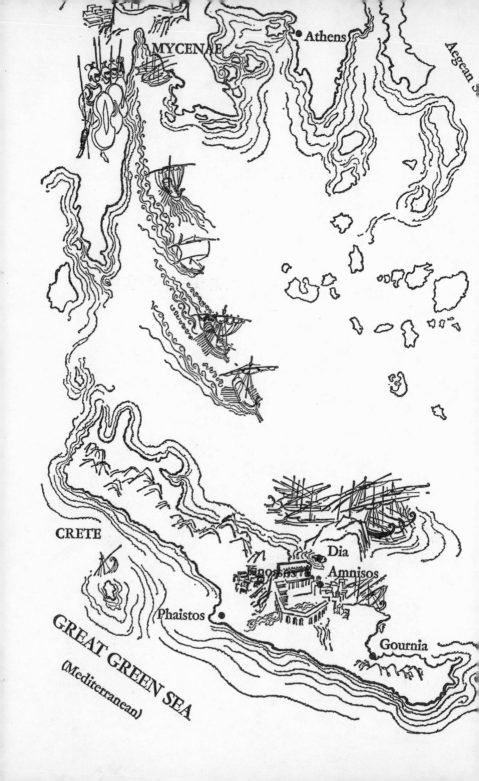

Athens

MYCENAE

Aegean S...

CRETE

GREAT GREEN SEA
(Mediterranean)

Knossos

Dia

Amnisos

Phaistos

Gournia

THE
TRAITOR QUEEN

Nancy Faulkner

DOUBLEDAY & COMPANY, INC.
GARDEN CITY, NEW YORK

25   50   100 MILES

Tom O'Sullivan

Library of Congress Catalog Card Number 63–16634
Copyright © 1963 by Anne I. Faulkner
All Rights Reserved
Printed in the United States of America
First Edition

FOR
EDWARD FENTON

CHAPTER
ONE

"By Poseidon, I'm cold!"

The voice was anonymous, coming from one of thirty young men and women standing where sea met land in the port town of Amnisos, awaiting the arrival of an embassy from the country of Mycenae to the Court of Minos, Priest-King of Crete.

A chorus of laughter and mocking words greeted the statement:

"Well! Imagine that."

"Who would have thought of such a thing?"

"Cold! What's cold?"

"Who said that?"

The same anonymous voice answered the last question. "I did. I, Drupos the Boxer. And I don't see anything funny about it."

Darkness was so thick about the huddling group faces were no more than blurred outlines. But Drupos recognized the voice of his cousin Thalamika when she said, "Be quiet, Drupos. We're all cold. You needn't make such a fuss about it."

She wished her cousin's mind were as active as his body. He was the best boxer in the House of the Priest-

King, admired and cheered wherever he went. He had dozens of friends who were always eager for his company and he was the idol of most of the girls in Knossos. But he wasn't loved for his brains, which seemed to most of his companions not to matter in so splendid an athlete.

He said, "Now see here, Thalamika, you don't need to . . ." and got no further, for another voice spoke into the night. "Hush! I think I hear oars."

They listened, but there was no sound beyond small restless movements among the watchers and the murmur of waves upon the sandy shore.

Thalamika pulled her light wool cloak closer about her throat. She wished she were back in the steep town of Knossos that joined the Palace of the Priest-King three miles above them. She should be abed in the house of her aunt, where she'd been living this year past, half-hearing her slave Chryses slide through the door bringing a brazier already glowing with fire.

How I hate the dark and cold, she thought, wondering if she would ever get over the fear that one day the Earth-Mother, the Great Goddess all Cretans worshiped, would destroy the sun in anger at some slight from her votaries. That was one trouble with being Priestess to The Goddess. The closer you came to Her secrets, the more you knew of Her jealousy and angers as well as Her love.

Why, Thalamika asked herself for the hundredth time, had her mother sent her to the Queen? She'd been happy at the southern palace at Phaistos, where her father was High Steward, until a year ago when her mother had told her curtly, without explanation, that she was going to the House of the Priest-King at Knossos to serve his Queen. Thalamika sighed, remembering how she had begged and stormed and, in the end, wept. But it hadn't done any good. Her mother had wept too, but she hadn't relented and, for the first time in her eighteen years, Thalamika had been forced to do something she really hated. Hated and dreaded, for she'd heard rumors about the Queen.

Myrtis, sister of King Lyssus of Mycenae, had come years ago to Crete to be Minos' Queen, and Thalamika knew many people wished her back in her brother's high fortress above the Plain of Argolis. They said harsh things about her but always behind their hands, whispering in hidden places because Minos would hear no evil of his beloved wife.

In the east, behind the small island of Dia which stood sentinel in the Bay of Amnisos, a milky whiteness was beginning to creep up the sky, foretelling the day. Thalamika forgot the Queen for a moment and drew in her breath in relief, feeling the sharp sting of the dawn cold in her throat but not caring now she knew light would return again to the earth. She spoke silently a small prayer of thanksgiving and greeting to the day, and went back to her musing, which at least helped to pass the waiting time.

Her dread of the Queen, she thought, had been well founded. Myrtis was mean-spirited, often cruel, always petulant. None of her handmaidens had any love for Myrtis. But Thalamika distrusted her too. She *knew* the Queen hated them all and would do them all damage if she could, but her knowledge was instinctive, beyond reasoning, and her logical mind was irked because she could find no reason for it.

She shrugged, dismissing puzzlement, concentrating on the more immediate irritation of this day. Why, why, *why* had Myrtis ordered half her ladies-in-waiting to get up in the middle of the night and come to welcome this goddess-cursed embassy from Mycenae? It was only seeking better trading privileges from Minos. It was the duty of the Priest-King's counselors to meet all embassies and welcome them in the name of Minos. Nobody had ever before thought it necessary to send boxers and bull leapers and maidens to the shore. It made no sense.

And, she told herself sternly, it made no sense to keep worrying away at such thoughts. She'd only make herself more miserable, adding anger and frustration to cold and boredom. The sun was showing its thin red rim above Dia, spraying the wide waters of the Great Green Sea with jewels. Thalamika set her attention on the miracle of the returning day, feeling at one with the sea and sky, the high hills and the fertile valleys as they stood forth in the growing light to greet the day in harmony.

"Look!" Drupos shouted and pointed toward Dia. "They're coming!"

Thalamika looked and saw, moving across the water turned a clear, deep blue, three thin, dark lines that each moment surged nearer and grew and took on height and breadth. Three ships, broad-beamed, high-beaked, sails stretched taut across the center masts, cut quickly through water that had lost its dawn stillness and was sending long, slow rollers toward the land.

One minute.

Two.

Three, and she could see clearly, in the brilliant light of the new sun, silhouettes of men standing upon the deck and sitting on the rowing thwarts. A minute more and the figures stood out clear and rounded, and she caught her breath.

"What kind of men *are* they, Drupos? Do they come from the Country of the Giants?"

Drupos laughed. "They're no giants, Thalamika, though the least of them is a head taller than most Cretans. You shouldn't be so surprised at their height. You're well accustomed to the tall Mycenean merchants in Crete. Look at the one who stands in the prow of the first ship. He must be the leader. Andrios says his name is Kretheus."

She had already seen him. He stood even taller than his companions. He wore, over a short yellow tunic and white drawers, a linen corselet covered with plates of some thin metal that shone in the sun. A conical helmet of boar's tusks with ivory cheek pieces framed a face whose most conspicuous feature, at this distance, was a carefully clipped blond beard. A bronze sword, broader and heavier than the familiar Cretan blade, hung at his side; and he held at arm's length, away from his body, carelessly as if he disdained its weight, a huge shield made of two leather circles connected by a narrow waistpiece and studded with metal.

She thought she'd never seen so splendid a man. She took a step forward toward the landing place to see him more closely, but Drupos' voice stopped her. "Poseidon!" he said. "They're armed! What can Lyssus be thinking of sending an armed band on a peaceful mission?"

His words angered her and she turned to him, her black eyes furious. "They're magnificent!" she said.

"Their leader is—must be—the very image of their mighty god Zeus."

"Don't be ridiculous, Thalamika. He's just an ordinary man, like any other, though a bit taller."

"You!" she said. "How can you say such stupid things? You—you're jealous, Drupos."

She looked at the slight, narrow-waisted boy beside her. His boxer's shoulders were broad, his arms and legs muscular. His skin was burned to the color of a fine bronze spearhead by years of living in the hot Cretan sun. He held himself with pride, and his eyes were bright with eagerness for living and sparkling with mischief. Yet, she thought, he might indeed and with justice envy such a man as Kretheus the Mycenean.

"Jealous of that great ox, Thalamika!" Drupos shouted with joyous laughter. "I could pin down his shoulders in two minutes. I'd wager he's more full of brawn than skill." He sobered then and added, "Just the same, it *is* shameful that a trade mission should come in arms to us, and I'll tell your 'god' so if I get the chance. What's more, you'd better be careful how you make eyes at him until you know more about him. I don't trust him and I'm sure Andrios will agree with me."

"Oh, Andrios!" The two words were enough to show her contempt. "Who cares what . . ." She interrupted herself as the young men and girls who'd been waiting so long began to form two parallel lines with a narrow way between. "Come on, Drupos. Don't just stand there. Get in line."

She leaned out and stretched her neck to see the beach. The sailors on each of the three ships had already stored masts and sails and were pulling the prows up onto the sand, well above the water line. The men of the embassy stepped to the shore and poured a libation to their gods and stood beside the boats, helmeted heads erect, bodies shield-covered from shoulder to ankle, spears grounded and pointing skyward in their right hands. Not a man moved except Kretheus, who, as the chief dignitaries of Crete came forward in gold and silver dress kilts, stepped out, and stood alone two paces ahead of his men in the exact center of their line.

Drupos jerked at Thalamika's cloak and warned her to stand straight and stop craning and staring, but she twitched away from him and moved her head angrily and he let her alone. He could almost envy the Myceneans, he thought. He'd been told they kept their women in the background and allowed them no part in the life of the country outside their homes. Little chance of such an arrangement with Cretan women. They had as many rights and privileges as the men, especially if they were Priestesses. He grinned to himself the next moment knowing he'd not really change the free give-and-take between the two sexes, no matter how much he might be annoyed now and then by his cousin. She was, he admitted, worse than most because she'd been spoiled from babyhood by her mother and father, who had no other children. In justice her waywardness wasn't her fault.

Thalamika edged a little out of line. It would take a while for all the greetings to be said. The Chief Potter was already holding out to Kretheus a cup as thin as an eggshell, patterned in black on a natural clay background. She recognized it as old and rare, made a long time ago in the region of Kamares. Minos himself must have some special concern for this embassy to offer so costly a gift to its leader.

Kretheus had laid aside his helmet and she could see that his hair curled crisply. He didn't wear it like the men of Crete, in long ringlets falling over the shoulder, but close-cropped. It gave him a look of strength and vigor which, together with his great height and the singular beauty and distinction of his features, set Thalamika's blood racing and her heart pounding with unaccustomed excitement. She wanted to run to him, to stand beside him and touch his hand and watch the play of his thoughts on his face.

She was so enthralled by the stranger she didn't notice a kilted figure coming toward her from the direction of the town until she felt a touch on her shoulder. She was startled and said, more sharply than she intended, "Oh, Andrios." Andrios bored her. He was much too serious. He hardly ever joined in the games and songs and dancing that helped make life in the Palace bearable for her. He seemed to her now ever duller than usual compared to the leader of the Myceneans.

"Go away!" she said crossly, and was startled when, instead of doing what she told him, he tightened his hand upon her arm so fiercely she winced with pain.

He hadn't meant to hurt her. He'd stiffened at the roughness in her voice and words and hadn't realized he'd dug viciously into her flesh. He'd wanted to talk to her if only for a moment, wanted to try to find in her company a little easing of the ache of his love for her. He'd never told her his love. Probably, he thought, he never would. He guessed she didn't like him and only suffered his presence for Drupos' sake. He'd not expected her to be overjoyed at his coming to talk to her. But neither had he expected her to be so actively hostile and he was angered and hurt. Besides, what was she doing, breaking the decorum of the greeting ceremonies by leaving her place and staring like a slave girl. What would the Myceneans think of her? He had no kindness for this embassy, coming in full armor to a peaceful country, but he didn't want Thalamika to appear badly in their eyes.

"Get back in line, Thalamika," he ordered her, not bothering to temper his quick anger with his usual gentleness. "You should know better than to behave in such an unseemly way when you're here as the Queen's representative."

She started to protest angrily but he wouldn't listen. "Yes, Thalamika, you have as much reason to behave properly as the others. More, since you're not only the Queen's handmaiden but a Priestess as well. You ought to be ashamed."

She was momentarily startled out of her absorption with the Myceneans. What had got into Andrios? Since she'd first met him in the House of the Priest-King a year ago, she'd never heard him speak in anger. Now his voice, though it was so quiet it didn't carry beyond her ears, whipped at her with such force she could almost feel it on her face. This was a new Andrios, and she wondered if she had, perhaps, misjudged him as a weakling. She stared at him, and it seemed to her she'd never really seen him before. She saw the snap in his black eyes that had always seemed too gentle for strength and noted the corded muscles in his back and arms. She wondered where he'd developed those muscles. He'd taken no part in any of the numerous athletic events at Knossos since she'd been here. He spent his time with the Priest-King, who was teaching him to administer the multiple affairs of the kingdom; or at one of the many shrines in the Palace serving the sacrifices as Cupbearer; or talking gravely with Sarpedon, Minos' twelve-year-old son, named they said for the brother of the first Minos who had ruled Crete in ages long lost to the memory of man. But this was a different Andrios and, perhaps, a more interesting one. She'd find out more about him from Drupos. Drupos would like nothing better than to talk about his hero.

Nevertheless, Andrios mustn't be allowed to think he could order her about and she lifted her eyebrows high and looked at him coldly. "You're not my keeper, Andrios the Cupbearer," she said. "I'll just ask you to leave me alone."

He didn't answer but withstood her stare briefly while his face went red then white. He turned away from her then and, still without speaking, went off in the direction he'd come.

She was surprised to find herself a little sorry she'd treated him so harshly, even a little ashamed of herself. But she'd no time for such thoughts now. The group on the shore was moving. The speeches of welcome must be over. There was a slight, confused bustle among the dignitaries and guests, and Thalamika stepped back to her place beside Drupos.

Slaves were passing along the lines. One of them handed her a garland. From the edge of the sea a double-pipe sounded a sweet, clear note. It was echoed at once by a lyre player and then taken up by all the Cretans and woven into a song of welcome. The men on the shore came walking slowly between the waiting lines of young men and girls, who scattered green boughs in their path and flung garlands of mauve anemones and red, small roses about their necks.

Thalamika looked at the garland in her own hand. It was a lovely thing, but it seemed too mean a thing for its purpose. She didn't intend to fling it carelessly, to land wherever The Goddess might direct. She meant to aim it squarely for Kretheus, who through some mischance was still ungarlanded. Maybe, then, if The Goddess were kind, he would turn his eyes from their fixed staring ahead and look at her.

He was no more than two paces away. She lifted the garland and, as he took one deliberate pace more, dropped it carefully over his shoulders. And he did look up. He saw her and smiled and settled the garland more securely and took the last pace that brought him abreast of her. He stopped so suddenly that the companion next behind him almost ran into him. Thalamika heard a muttered curse, but it might have come from the Country of the Dead so remote it seemed from the small island of delight where she stood—or thought she stood—alone with Kretheus.

She saw the deep blue of his eyes, smiling a little, and his astonished pleasure at her beauty. She had, all her life, been accustomed to see such looks in men's eyes, but until now she'd given it little thought, content to accept her face without vanity as the gift of The Goddess. Now she was glad of her beauty if it brought him pleasure.

He inclined his head toward her and said, speaking loud and clear with a voice that had in it a harsh under-

tone for all its surface sweetness, "I thank you, my lady."
She thought he was going to say more but he stood a
moment longer and, in that moment, whispered one
word, for her alone: "Later."

She wondered if she had heard aright and knew in her
leaping heart she had. She turned in her place to follow
in the wake of the embassy, singing with the rest, through
the town of Amnisos and across the River Kairatos and up
the long, steep hill, where the great Palace of Minos at
Knossos glittered in the sparkling, light, moving air of
Crete.

CHAPTER
TWO

Thalamika did not see Kretheus again that day. Words had run about the sprawling House of the Priest-King, buzzing in shrines and kitchens, in halls and corridors, in guardhouse and court, storage rooms and workshops of artisans. Words were spoken by slaves and guardsmen, fresco painters and potters, jewel cutters and unguent boilers and merchants chaffering over their wares in the West Court. Words beat at doors and whispered down light shafts until the tale of Thalamika's ill-bred behavior reached the Queen's apartment and, at last, the Queen's ears.

The Queen's chair had been placed near the light well. The gardens and walls that edged the top of the hill above the river were gay and fragrant with new spring flowers, and the breeze from Mount Dichte was pleasant in the warm morning. The Queen was tall, but stooped. Flabby fat almost concealed the good bone structure of her long face, except for the nose, which was high-ridged and prominent. Her hair, once the color of oak leaves in autumn, was streaked with white and lacked luster and her blue eyes were faded and held a look of discontent. She wore a scarlet Cretan dress that seemed somehow to set off all the worst features of her figure and looked as if it should have belonged to someone else. She had in her hands a piece of fine Egyptian linen and, beside her chair, a wide, shallow bowl decorated with spirals, full of many-colored threads, but she was not attending to her embroidery. She sat musing, rather, and a beginning smile brought a little of her old beauty to her face. Two of her companions whispered nearby. They were older than her Cretan handmaidens—women who had come with her when, as a girl of sixteen, she'd been sent by her father to be Queen to Minos, Priest-King of Crete. "She's happy," the women whispered one to another. "She's thinking of home," and they sighed, for they too had often been sick for the great hill palace at Mycenae and the wide-flowing Plain of Argolis.

Two Cretan girls, freshly bathed and dressed in long, flounced skirts embroidered in clear, rich colors, came into the Queen's Hall and took their places on stools a little distance from their mistress. For a time they sat quietly, waiting for the Queen to begin the day's talk. When she kept silence, the girls began to whisper together in their turn, not heeding the sharp looks from the older women.

At first the Queen paid them little attention. Her mind was, in truth, far from Knossos and the island that had been a prison to her for so many, far-stretching years. She saw nothing to admire in the great Palace and the city which many people called the most beautiful in the world, nor found comfort for her exile among the peace-loving people of Crete. She wanted for this day to escape from all of it in memories of her homeland, made more vivid by the coming of Kretheus, whom she had not yet seen. What word would he bring of her brother, his lord?

The Cretan girls giggled, breaking into her reveries. By the Great Goddess these Cretans worshiped, the Queen thought, there was no peace in Knossos, not even in her own apartments. Could she never be free of the constant chaffering and nattering of feckless girls who would not learn to be silent? That's what came, she supposed, of worshiping that unpleasant female deity, that goddess they called the Lady of this and the Lady of that and the Mistress of the other thing, until the very multiplication of names was a confusion in the mind. By any name their goddess could be as revengeful and cruel as Zeus himself, who had at least the excuse of being a proper male god. Pah upon their lady!

In spite of herself the Queen shuddered and made the sign against evil. She didn't understand this worship of the dark and mysterious Earth Mother but, for all her scorn and disbelief, the Queen wondered if the dreaded SHE could search out and punish thoughts of a woman alien to the little, dark-browed Cretans.

The Queen tried to recapture her mood of happy remembering and, because she couldn't, turned in anger toward the two girls and shouted at them. "Irata and Amphidora, if you must talk, speak your thoughts aloud to me. What you say in my hall, it's my right to hear."

"It—it's nothing, O Queen," Amphidora said, "not of enough importance for troubling the Queen's ears." Amphidora was a gentle person and, though she was trembling before the Queen's anger, had no wish to make trouble for anyone.

"SPEAK, girl!" Myrtis' voice was shrill. "Or would you rather be whipped for disobedience?"

"It—it's—just . . ." Amphidora tried to explain, but fear caught in her throat and stopped the words.

"Fool!" the Queen said, "take hold of yourself or . . ."

"If the Queen pleases!" Irata interrupted softly. She wasn't afraid of the Queen's anger and she rather enjoyed stirring up a beehive of confusion for the companions of the Queen's Household.

"Well!"

"Only this, O Queen. Amphidora and I were talking of the new embassy and of the behavior of your hand-maiden at Amnisos this morning."

"And what *of* the behavior of my handmaiden? *And* which one?"

"If the Queen wishes to hear the tale," Irata began, and was interrupted with acid mimicry.

"If the Queen wishes to hear the tale! If the Queen wishes . . . ! Is the Queen mad then? Of course the Queen wishes to hear it. Hasn't the Queen been trying this long time to hear it?"

Irata told her then of Thalamika and Kretheus, and watched rising anger redden the Queen's face and was glad for that sight. Of all the women of the Queen's chamber she disliked Thalamika most, and was spitefully pleased to do her an injury.

When the story was finished there was a time of silence while the Queen struggled to reduce her spleen. When, at last, she could bring out words coherently, without spluttering, she said, "Go away. Both of you. Out of my sight. And send Thalamika to me without delay."

Amphidora, as soon as they were in the corridor, began

to chide Irata for bringing trouble to Thalamika. "Be quiet, Amphidora," Irata ordered. "What's Thalamika to you that you should risk the Queen's anger? Our fine mistress would gladly have had you beaten with whips. And it wouldn't do any good for your father, even if he is Chief Potter and favored above most men, to go to Minos. Minos will believe nothing but good of the Queen, and small wonder since she always puts on for him that sweet face, simpering whenever she's in his sight. Let Thalamika take care of herself, and if anything evil comes to her, remember she alone is responsible. If she'd behaved herself properly this morning, she'd not have given Myrtis any reason for anger."

Amphidora sniffled. "Why do you hate Thalamika so much, Irata?" she asked. "She's never done you any harm and she's usually kind. She's a little headstrong but she doesn't go out of her way to hurt people."

"Oh, stop sniveling and go bathe your face, Amphidora, and leave Thalamika to me since you're so soft-hearted about her," Irata said by way of answer, and left her gentle companion.

But it was nearly an hour before Thalamika went to the Queen. Irata found her quickly enough but didn't dare speak to her. Thalamika was in the Sanctuary of the Central Court, offering the daily bloodless sacrifice of fruit and flowers at the shrine of the Lady of the Labyrinth. No one, not even the Priest-King himself, would disturb this daily ritual for fear of the anger of The Goddess.

Irata sent a slave to tell the Queen of the delay. She herself had no wish to bring upon her head her mistress's displeasure. She watched a group of children playing knucklebones in the middle of the Court, wishing she had brought a palm leaf to protect her face from the morning sun. It was overwarm for the Month of Seafaring. Who would have thought to guard against sunburn so soon after the winter storms?

The great Court was full of movement. Royal officers came and went, hurrying to and fro upon the King's business. Their kilts, crimson and blue and gold, beneath the wide, tight belts of bronze or silver set with precious stones, flashed in the sun and set off their sunburned legs and arms, torsos and faces against the background of dazzling white stones of the Palace walls. Now and again one of them stopped in his hurrying way to watch the children and smile at their small, keen pleasures. The blue-black bodies of the Palace Guard of Nubians from the far-distant desert beyond the Land of the Pharaohs shone with oil and sweat, as they stood their watch at the doors of the Throne Room and Sanctuary and beside the wide-shadowed steps that led to the formal reception hall on the top story of the Palace of Minos.

Usually Irata would have smiled at the scene, but today she was bored and irritated because she had to wait in the sun for Thalamika when she might have spent her unexpected free time watching the bull leapers practicing outside their Court. They had already begun intensive training, readying themselves for the Bull Games to be held in honor of The Goddess and Her Consort Poseidon when the harvests were gathered at midsummer.

What was keeping the girl? Surely there'd been time enough to complete the sacred rites a dozen times.

Irata walked half the length of the long Court. Should

$17.89

she go further to see how the fresco of the charging bull at the north entrance to the Palace was progressing? Before she could decide she heard music behind her and knew the rites were finally over and turned and started back along the Court.

She didn't take her eyes from the entrance to the Sanctuary. It would take her several minutes to return to it, and if she should miss Thalamika she might have to waste more time searching here and there among the endless halls and courts and workshops. It was well that she watched, for Thalamika came out almost at once and hurrying. She was rearranging the fillet that bound the knot of black hair at the nape of her neck and squinting against the sudden sun glare of the Court.

Irata, in spite of the day's warmth, began to run, calling as she came, "Oh, Thalamika!"

Thalamika turned and saw her and stood still, raising her hand in acknowledgment of the call. She didn't like Irata and wouldn't waste any words on her. What was she doing here, in any case? This was her morning to sit with the Queen and listen to endless complaints about the land of Crete and everything in it. Poseidon take the Woman of Mycenae!

Thalamika shivered. Whatever had made her call upon Poseidon? He held, if possible, more dread for her mind than The Goddess in her moods of anger for if Poseidon took offense at mortals, he lashed the waters and shook the firm earth to destroy it. She wished her mind had not betrayed her into thinking his name.

"Stay, O Thalamika," Irata called, "I have a message for you from the Queen."

Thalamika waited and Irata came up to her, panting a

little and speaking in spurts of words between pants. "You're in trouble, my girl. The Queen has heard of your behavior at the beach this morning and she doesn't like it. You're to go to her at once. And I'm glad I'm not in your shoes, for she's very angry and spoke of the whip."

Thalamika was furious. Who could have told the Queen what had happened in the dawn time? Irata hadn't been at the shore. Had it been Andrios? She dismissed that thought at once, for though Andrios might be dull and simple-minded he was no tattletale. She wanted to ask Irata but wouldn't give her that satisfaction. She willed her face to calm and hid her feelings behind it and turned toward the Queen's Hall, not looking again at Irata.

Thalamika cut diagonally across the Court, not hurrying, and deliberately waited a minute at the top of the broad stone staircase that led to the lower story and the entrance to the Queen's apartments. It was a lovely thing, that staircase, broad and graceful with watercourses set beside it to take off the rain dropped by the heavy storms of winter and carry it to a cistern at the bottom of the hill. She could feel the bustle of the Court behind her and wished she didn't have to leave it. She didn't look forward to the coming interview. She had no fear of the Queen, for, as a Priestess, she was protected from the worst of her anger, but she had since this morning been living in a happy dream of Kretheus the godlike, and she knew the Queen's unpleasantness would break into it.

Would break into it! By the Dove of the Goddess, that mood was already shattered! Irata had done that. Best get the next part over.

She went down the stairs and stopped at the entrance to the Queen's chambers to unfasten the broad straps over her ankles and take off the soft leather shoes, which she handed to a slave who waited at the door. Her silver anklets chimed softly as she made her way through a maze of rooms and corridors that would have bewildered anyone not long accustomed to the pattern of the Palaces of Crete. She wished with all her mind she need never see Myrtis again, but wishing would get her nowhere. She sighed and straightened her blue jacket with the puffed sleeves. She had come, at last, to the Queen's own hall.

The doors were open, fitted flat into bays on either side of the entrance. She could see clearly into the room, and as always her breath caught at the beauty of the frescoed walls with their clear-colored frieze of dancers and, upon the ceiling, pictures of lotus and papyrus so real you almost felt they were living flowers.

The Queen was walking about the room. Her back was toward the door, but no one needed to see the face to guess her anger. The two serving women from Mycenae were huddled together on the bright cushions that softened the stone bench running the length of the room. The sun's rays, striking through the light well, just touched their faces and they looked frightened and miserable, though it was seldom they felt even the edge of the Queen's wrath.

"Who is this girl that she thinks she can keep the Queen waiting as if she were a slave? They are all alike, these Cretans, and I shall destroy them." The Queen turned toward her frightened serving women, and her voice squeaked as it rose higher and higher. She had forgotten the first cause of her anger, and all her venom was centered now upon Thalamika's tardiness and her long-held hatred of the people of Crete. "Do you hear me and heed what I say," she went on. *"I shall destroy them.* I, Myrtis of Mycenae, if Zeus will send his aid, will have vengeance upon this land for the slights its people have laid upon me."

Thalamika touched the stiff loop of material knotted at her shoulder that marked her as Priestess of the Lady of the Labyrinth. What was the Woman of Mycenae saying? Destroy the Cretans! She must be mad. Thalamika shivered a little. Before this was over she would need the protection of The Lady. She took a step into the room and stood clear of the door bays. She held herself very straight and spoke clearly and firmly and with full formality.

"You sent for me, O Queen, and I, Thalamika, Daughter of Kalmia of Phaistos, have come."

The Queen turned about as if the harmless house snake had suddenly and unexpectedly bitten her. For a moment she glared at the slight figure defying her from the doorway. When she spoke her voice was so low it hardly carried across the room, but it was as menacing as the stillness at the heart of a great wind.

"So! You've come, Thalamika, in your own good time. And will you tell me why you've kept your Queen waiting the twelfth part of a day?"

"I was about the business of The Goddess, O Queen."

"The Goddess. The Goddess. And do you think your goddess can save you from the Queen's anger?" She turned to the serving woman. "Call the slave of the whips, Thera."

One of the women on the bench got up and started to the door. She sidled toward it slowly, along the wall, giving the Queen a wide berth. Thalamika didn't move. She'd forgotten her momentary fear and had begun to enjoy herself. The Queen, when angered enough, was likely to forget Cretan customs, and Thalamika was about to triumph over her mistress and knew it.

"You needn't send for the slave, O Queen. It's forbidden even to the Queen to touch in anger a Priestess of the Lady of the Labyrinth." She paused a moment then went on, not able to keep from being deliberately insulting. "Indeed, it's a pity the Queen can think of no way except the whip to win the allegiance of her handmaidens. In all places in Crete except the Queen's Hall, the whip is kept for slaves and the base born."

She felt safe and secure under the protection of The Goddess. Her whole body was rejoicing in the sight of the Woman of Mycenae, who was pale and trembling.

But the next moment Thalamika was herself trembling, though she hoped the Queen was too agitated to notice. She'd thought suddenly of a way the Queen could punish her. The Queen could send her back to Phaistos. Yesterday she would have welcomed such banishment, in spite of the disgrace. Today—today it would mean she wouldn't ever see Kretheus the Mycenean again, and the very fear of it was enough to set her quaking.

The Queen's mouth was working as she tried to find breath to speak. Thalamika looked down. She must turn her mind from the thought of banishment. What if The Lady were gamesome and took her thoughts and sent them flying into the Queen's mind? She held herself tight and tried to stop thinking.

She relaxed slowly as the Queen spoke. "You, Thalamika, will learn to come quickly to my command. You
will learn that I, too, can think of other punishments for
upstart girls who know nothing of proper courtesy. Now
hear me. You will from this day, until I give you leave
to stop, leave your uncle's house and live with the bull
leapers, sharing their hard beds and coarse food. What's
more, your time in my service will be doubled from
henceforth."

Thalamika half-turned away to hide the laughter she
couldn't keep out of her face. This Woman of Mycenae
was indeed a fool. This, except for the extra time to be
spent in her presence, was no punishment at all. How
could Myrtis fail to know, after these many years at the
House of the Priest-King, that the bull leapers were the
envy of every young man and young woman in Crete?
To live with them, if it were possible, even for a day
would be a joy and delight. Not that there was any
chance such a thing would come about. The Queen
couldn't command the bull leapers. They weren't likely
to permit any outsider to share their quarters in their special Court while they were training for the harvest games.
They were jealous of their special state. But she wouldn't
tell the Queen so. Let her learn it for herself, if learn it
she did. She took little interest in anything beyond her
own Hall.

"And now," the Queen said, "get out of my sight,
Thalamika the Discourteous, and don't come near my per-
son when you do my service. Remember that and . . .
GO."

Thalamika made a low bow and went.

CHAPTER
THREE

Thalamika took her shoes from the slave and strapped them on. She'd have to hurry. The interview had taken too much time from her carefully planned day. She ran up the broad stairway and down the length of the Central Court, almost colliding with a fat Egyptian merchant, who shook his fist at her back muttering curses. At the top of the flight of stairs leading to the vestibule at the southern entrance to the Palace, she stopped to recover her breath before she went on, more slowly, along a corridor with walls covered by frescoes showing a procession of young men and girls carrying the sacred vessels used in the worship of The Goddess. One of the cupbearers of the picture was so much like Andrios she always expected the painted figure to speak. No wonder, for the father of Andrios was Master of the Frescoes for the Priest-King and had, no doubt, used his son as a model when the designs were lined out with fine thread in the wet plaster.

She wouldn't look at the fresco now. She'd no wish to think about Andrios. She'd had enough of solemnity for one day, and it was impossible to think of him in any other way. She turned her mind toward the afternoon when Minos, the Priest-King, would come to the Reception Hall above the Throne Room to welcome the embassy from Mycenae. But before then she, with the other younger Priestesses, would salute The Goddess on behalf of the guests in the dancing place. She was sure she could manage to be named leader of the dancers, and so Kretheus the Mycenean, who would have the place of honor beside Minos, couldn't fail to notice her.

She ducked down yet another stairway, narrow and steep, and left the Palace precincts and went down the street toward the river and to her uncle's house, which clung to the hillside like a snail. Carrying her shoes, she passed quickly through the ground-floor room, empty except for a stone bench, uncushioned, along one side and a carved stone lamp taller than her head that lighted the room and sweetened it with perfumed oil. She passed the closed door to the house shrine, wondering if the house snake had been properly fed today, and called for her slave as she went up the stairs. She was already half out of her dress by the time she came to her own quarters.

Chryses was waiting. "You're late, O Mistress," she said reprovingly. "I've twice had to replenish the brazier for your bath."

"I couldn't help it, Chryses, so don't scold. The Queen sent for me when I'd finished the Sacrifice."

Chryses sniffed. She had no love for the Queen.

"I couldn't help it, truly, Chryses. Help me off with this dress. I've little enough time as it is to get ready for the dancing."

"Dancing, is it?" Chryses said. "And your finest dress not yet back from the fuller's, where I sent it when you spilled the honey through gaping at some young man."

"Well, go and get it. Quickly. I'll wear no second best today with the embassy from Mycenae to be honored. What men they are, Chryses! So tall and strong. Such beards on their faces. Their leader, Kretheus, is more god than man."

Chryses made a face. She hated all Myceneans. "You'd better take your mind from such as he, O Mistress," she said, and Thalamika wondered if there were a conspiracy to spoil her interest in the Mycenean. "You'll get nothing but sorrow from Mycenean men," Chryses went on before Thalamika could protest. "I say it. I, Chryses of the Shore Folk. And who has a better right? But for the thieving, raiding men of Mycenae, wouldn't I even now be free as you, though still of less account since my father was a simple man?"

"Do be quiet, Chryses," Thalamika said sharply. "I've heard the story of the raid upon your father's land and the enslavement of all your family by Mycenean pirates a hundred times. I've no time for it now. Besides you're not so badly off here. You've little cause to moan and weep in this household, where you eat better and drink better wine than ever you had in your little Athens. And Kretheus is no pirate but a prince in Argolis. Now go on to the fuller's for my dress."

"Your bath," Chryses began, but Thalamika cut her short. "I'll manage my own bath for once. Hurry!"

Chryses left, muttering. She knew too well what happened when Thalamika managed her own bath. Water over everything. Clothes scattered from one end of the bedroom to the other end of the bathroom and covered with unguents and eye paint and face paint besides. No matter. There was no sense in arguing. Arguing only made the girl more stubborn and like as not would gain Chryses nothing better than a box upon the ears. Spoiled that girl was. Plain spoiled and wayward. And no wonder, the way her mother doted on her. How would *she* like being a slave, ordered about, with no life of her own, no freedom ever? Chryses shrugged and went out to the Palace fuller.

Three hours later Thalamika examined herself carefully in the polished bronze mirror Chryses held for her. Her black hair was bound with a fillet of amethyst and gold except where it escaped in carefully arranged ringlets over her shoulder. She tightened the bronze hair pins once more. This would be no wild, ecstatic dance of invocation to The Goddess. It would be controlled and stately, honoring the Lady of the Labyrinth and the embassy, and it wouldn't do to have the pins loosen and leave her hair unbound. Satisfied that they were tight, she turned her attention to her face. It was as carefully tended as her hair, just enough scarlet, powdered saffron on her lips to heighten the clear white of her skin; just enough black on her eyebrows and at the corners of her eyes to underscore their brightness. She needed no one to warn her not to overdo the paint for lips and eyes as some of the girls did, distracting from their beauty by lack of restraint. Her face would do.

She applied perfumed oil to her earlobes and the dark wings of hair over her ears and got up from the stool before her dressing table and checked her dress. The ankle-length skirt was white and bell-shaped, stiffened so that it stood out evenly all round her. The bodice, white with scarlet threads woven into an intricate pattern, was open from throat to narrow waist over a thin chemisette. She pushed up the short sleeves to accentuate their puff; held out her hand for her high-heeled shoes, the leather dyed scarlet to match the decoration on her bodice; and moved to the door, conscious of her own grace, glad she didn't need to wear the stiff gold stays so many women used to control their overfat bodies.

She had to walk the full length of the Palace to reach the dancing place and she was glad she'd allowed enough time to walk slowly and with dignity, for the corridors and courts were swarming with the hundreds of people who lived and worked in the House of the Priest-King. At the door of the Sanctuary, where she'd helped with the Sacrifice this morning, she joined the other girls waiting for the Chief Priestess, who came almost at once from the shrine wearing a flat hat topped by the figure of a dove. A small snake, sacred to The Lady in her guise of Goddess of the Underworld and of Death, was wreathed about each arm. Thalamika managed to get near enough to her to whisper a request to be made leader of the dancing. The Chief Priestess, old and wise, looked at her carefully and nodded. Thalamika was, she thought, the best of the younger attendants on The Goddess; more careful than the others of decorum and restraint in her dress and her ways. More important, she was much the best dancer of them all, and today of all days the dance must go well. The Priest-King had made it plain they must impress this embassy from Mycenae, though why she couldn't say since the Myceneans, with their myriad gods, chiefly masculine and warlike, were not likely to care much for dances in honor of a foreign goddess, no matter how much revered and worshiped in her own home. Still, Thalamika would do them honor as leader, for she was a lovely thing to watch and obedient and gracious in her service to The Lady, though accounted wayward and spoiled in secular life. She'd learn in time, and meanwhile she would lead the dance with grace and precision today.

The Central Court was clear now, and the Chief Priestess signaled the votaries and walked toward the north entrance and from there to the dancing place. The rising tiers of stone seats for the audience were crowded. The sacred pillar, set at the edge of the theater, was crowned with a double-bladed bronze ax, incised with decorations of olive leaves, a representation in miniature of the huge Labrys used in the blood sacrifices. As she walked beneath it, Thalamika looked up at it and said in her heart, "Blessed be the Lady of the Labyrinth."

The Chief Priestess led the dancers onto the smooth pavement of the dancing place and, facing the pillar, lifted the snakes toward it, invoking the good will of The Goddess. A boy, hidden in a grove of pine trees new-tipped with spring-green needles, struck a chord on a lyre and was answered at once by other lyre players. The men and women upon the stone seats sang, as if they were one person, the hymn to the Lady of the Labyrinth, invoking her presence, praying she would bring fertility to the crops and the flocks.

As the song reached its most solemn point, Thalamika heard above her head a fluttering of sound and looked up and saw a white dove that circled once about the pillar before it settled upon the staff of the double ax. A sudden stillness in her mind blotted out the singing, which rose triumphantly as all the audience saw the dove and recognized in it the presence of The Goddess Herself, who had heard their prayers and come among them.

Thalamika, with awe and reverence, felt her spirit uplifted. She forgot Kretheus the Mycenean, forgot the Queen, forgot the glory of the day about her, forgot even herself. She was no longer Thalamika the Beautiful, daughter of Kalmia of Phaistos. She was all Priestess, dedicated to the service of The Lady, here to do Her honor in the sacred dance.

She felt a tremor that started in her mind and flowed through her, pulsing to the music, setting her body in motion. Her right arm raised upward and outward. Her left hand, of itself, stretched behind her to take the right hand of the first dancer and she stepped out upon the pavement in the beginning figure of the dance.

Above her unseeing eyes the people made a splendor of color, a frescoed background for two central figures. Minos, the Priest-King, sat hunched a little, like a toad; small, crouched, his overfed belly extending grotesquely beneath his tightly belted waist. But no one gave a second glance to the middle-aged body, for his face, still beautiful in spite of his age, was the face of a man whose mind was as lean and active as his body was slothful and gross. This Minos, trained and accustomed from his earliest childhood to rule, would allow no smallest swerving from his decrees and would give justice according to the laws to all who obeyed the laws. He was the ruler of his people, the chief representative upon earth of The Goddess and Poseidon Her Consort. He was full of dignity and intelligence, strong upon the land and upon the Great Green Sea which his warships controlled, rich, powerful, secure in confidence in himself.

Beside him, Kretheus, Prince of Mycenae, sat nearly half again as tall; young, arrogant, a little bored but stonestill as courtesy dictated. His tunic, white and gold, fell softly across the stone, accentuating the grace of his seated body. His beard was newly trimmed and combed, and his hair glistened with oil. Few of the people about him could take their eyes from him, but if he felt their curious scrutiny he gave no sign. He was watching the girl who led the dance, the girl who'd thrown him a garland this morning. She was, he thought, already spellbound by him and he was glad to have it so. Since she led the dance she must be a person of some consequence and, in spite of her unseemly boldness, even because of it, he could perhaps mold her to the hidden purposes of his King. He'd seek her out, he thought, and foster her interest and play upon it. But, he frowned, she didn't seem to be even aware of him now. Somehow he must draw her eyes to him. By Zeus, she was beautiful! And she danced like a goddess herself.

The music of the lyres quickened for the climax of the dance. The line of Priestesses, dipping and swaying in rhythm to the music followed gracefully and without effort the intricate patterns Thalamika improvised for them. The Chief Priestess, watching from the edge of the paved way, nodded to herself. Her old and faded eyes shone with pleasure at Thalamika's inventiveness. The Priest-King would be pleased. He might even send a gift of gold or jewels to the House of the Priestess.

The dancers had circled the far end of the theater and were coming back for their final and most elaborate figure before the audience. The Chief Priestess was glad. She tired easily these days. She looked up at the pillar. The dove was no longer on her perch. No matter. The Goddess had graced them for a while, for long enough. She closed her eyes, aching with watching so much movement in the white glare of the sun. Thalamika would bring them off with the proper decorum. No need to worry now. The Old Priestess dozed in the sun.

A rush of sound from the seats penetrated Thalamika's concentration and reached the part of her mind that had become empty with the coming of the dove. It seemed to her that every member of the watching crowd had drawn breath at once in a gasp of—what? Horror? Fear? What had happened while she was Goddess-filled? What could have gone wrong?

The rhythm of the dance faltered and she tightened her muscles to command control from those behind her and felt the rhythm return to perfection. Reassured that no error of the dancers would displease The Goddess and bring Her wrath upon them all, she glanced quickly at the people above her and almost sounded her dismay at what she saw. Kretheus was looking steadily at her; looking at her as if she were any maiden and not a Priestess in the performance of her cult duties; willing her eyes, she thought, to meet his. And even as she struggled to keep, against the impulsion of his will, her mind and body concentrated upon the dance, she saw he'd taken the circlet of olive leaves from his head and raised it toward her, saw him about to speak and knew terror that he would profane with sacrilege the presence of The Goddess. Surely he must know no mortal should address a Priestess of The Lady in a ritual dance. She must get away quickly. She raised the tempo of her movement, ignoring the lyres which sought to follow now rather than lead the dance. But even as she did so she knew there was no need. For Andrios, sitting directly behind Kretheus, grasped the wrist below the circlet in one hand and put his other upon Kretheus' shoulder, letting it weigh there as if it had been molded of bronze. At the same time the Young Prince Sarpedon, seated beside Andrios, put his small, strong hand firmly over the mouth of the Mycenean.

Thalamika led the line of Priestesses across the dancing place toward the grove of pine trees that would mask their exit. All sense of dedication had left her. She was concerned only with the mechanics of movement, with the need to keep her trembling legs performing the few remaining measures with dignity. The grove looked an endless distance away, but she kept her eyes steadily upon it, and at last felt the stone pavement give way to the soft crunch of pine needles.

She leaned against the bole of an ancient tree and let it support her while the trembling gradually went away. She half-heard snatches of sentences as the others came into the safe gloom of the grove and put away their sanctity and began to talk excitedly of the dance.

". . . see the face of the Young Prince . . ."

"Did *you* see how the white-robed Mycenean . . ."

". . . was it Thalamika . . ."

Thalamika paid little attention. Her own sense of shock and anger at Kretheus was passing with the trembling. He had surely meant no dishonor. How could he have known their customs? He lived far across the Great Green Sea and honored other gods, probably in other ways. Perhaps she should join the talk about her and plead his innocence for him, since he couldn't make his own explanations. Or perhaps it would be better to keep her silence and go nearer and listen to what they were saying, the better to warn him about the temper of the women who served in the House of the Priest-King. She pushed away from the support of her tree and started toward the group which stood a little apart from her, but a shout of applause from the dancing place, where the jugglers were entertaining the people, releasing gaiety after the solemn spell of the dance, stopped her hearing. When the sound died away the knot of young women had already untangled itself, most of them hurrying through the grove to places where they could watch the antic performers. Thalamika heard only a few final sentences. "You couldn't know, Thalia, because you've been here such a short time. But of course Andrios could stop the spear carrier. Andrios has the strength of ten men. He was the best bull leaper of all the Companions of the Bull Court before he was chosen as Cup-bearer. He wrestled more bulls to the ground than any other leaper in our time, and that without getting so much as a single horn scratch. Look at the muscles in his shoulders next time you see him, and notice his arms and thighs. Warrior-proud Kretheus had better . . ."

The two girls moved further away, out of Thalamika's hearing. She stood where she was, surprise and anger mixed in her mind.

Andrios a bull leaper? She could scarcely credit it. She couldn't imagine him among the young men and girls of the Bull Court—fearless, strength-proud, full of laughter and song. She'd known many of them well at

Phaistos, and she couldn't picture the solemn Andrios as one of them.

Anger against him surged into her mind. Why had he been so rough with Kretheus? Couldn't he have warned the stranger, quietly and with gentleness becoming a courtier of the House of the Priest-King? He knew Kretheus was a stranger and probably ignorant of their customs. Why had Andrios seen fit to force him into his seat? To lay upon a guest the indignity of his strong hands? To lead the Young Prince to cover a guest's mouth?

Another shout came from the dancing place. The jugglers would be done. The watchers would be leaving their places, hurrying back to the Palace for their afternoon resting time. She'd go on ahead and wait for Andrios by the pillars of the North Porch, for he would be sure to come that way.

He saw her when he was still a distance away. She beckoned him and he raised his hand in greeting and spoke to young Sarpedon, sending him running off toward the Potters' Workshops. She smiled a little, thinking of the boy. He would make a proper Priest-King some day. He was like a dragonfly shining in the sun. He never walked but darted about as if to be alive were so joyful a thing he wouldn't miss a moment of it. She must admit Andrios had done much for him. When she'd first seen the boy he'd been awkward and shy. But then Minos had appointed Andrios as his companion and tutor, and the Young Prince had blossomed into this creature of the upper air. Strange that Andrios . . .

Andrios had reached the porch while she'd been thinking. His face was alight and the laughter in his eyes made them outsparkle the amethyst sealstone that hung about his neck on a golden wire.

The laughter tugged at her and she felt laughter growing in her to meet it. She'd never seen Andrios gay. He spoke to her with joy, without a trace of the care and seriousness she'd come to think the marks of his mind. "You waited for me, Thalamika!" he said and took her hands.

At the strength of his touch she forgot laughter, his and hers, and remembered only her anger and tugged against his hold. He released her hands instantly, and the light went from his eyes as if a window had been covered against the sun. She felt a moment of loss but she ignored it and it went away as she answered formally, "Yes, O Andrios, I waited for you. I saw you using your strength against the shield-bearing Kretheus, a guest in our land and in the House of the Priest-King, and I wanted to know why you were so discourteous."

She saw anger brighten the blank eyes and go out of them as he controlled it. "He was about to profane the dance, Thalamika," he said mildly. "I had to stop him."

"Did you think he was a wild bull to be thrown for the sacrifice, O Andrios, that you must show your great strength against him?"

"Would you have wanted me to permit sacrilege, Thalamika?"

"Oh, sacrilege!" She stamped her foot on the hard stone of the porch. "By the Blade of the Labrys, how could he have intended sacrilege when he has just come to Knossos and is certainly ignorant of our customs? You're lying, Andrios. You just wanted to show your strength. . . ."

She stopped before the look of anger in his face. His slight, strong body was stiff and tight with it. He held his hands rigidly at his sides, but his kilts were shaking with the shaking of his fury so that the woven blue lilies seemed to come alive upon the white cloth. He drew in his breath harshly and said, "I do not lie, O Thalamika of Phaistos. I, Andrios the Cupbearer, do—not—lie."

Then, before she could speak any of the things that crowded her mind, he turned abruptly and went away from her, almost running in his haste to be gone.

CHAPTER
FOUR

Next morning Thalamika awoke early and lay thinking
of yesterday while she waited for Chryses to make her
ready for the day. She felt a little foolish at the way she'd
railed at Andrios. She shouldn't have called him a liar.
He'd never trifled with the truth, and if he had laid
hands on Kretheus it must have been because he believed the Mycenean had deliberately planned to com-
mit sacrilege. Though she had no great fondness for
Andrios, he'd done her no harm and she didn't want to
quarrel with him. She'd ask his forgiveness, explain
she'd been overwrought from the dance, and he would
smile at her. She'd like to see his eyes fill again with
the sudden laughter that had delighted her yesterday.
She wondered, as she thought about these things, why
she cared about the laughter in his eyes. Probably because she was Cretan and therefore was born to enjoy
laughter.

She stretched her small body in the bed and turned
her thoughts to the morning ahead. It would be a good
morning—once she'd finished her service to the Queen.
Already the frieze of lilies on the walls of her room was
taking on color from the rosy-red shaft coming through

the light well. Later she was going with Drupos and
some of his companions to meet Philona, her friend and
Drupos' beloved, who would return today to her father's
house in Amnisos. Thalamika wondered how Philona,
who had not been part of her father's household since
she was a baby, was feeling at this homecoming. Probably forlorn and uncertain. Well, no matter. It wouldn't
take long to make new friends. She was a happy soul,
warmhearted and easy to know.

Thalamika threw back the covers and left the bed.
She wouldn't wait for Chryses. She'd make her own toi-
let and be ready all the earlier to go to the Queen's Hall
and get it over with. She was bored with the very thought
of the Queen, and wondered how long the Woman of
Mycenae would demand twice the usual time. Never
mind. At least the Queen demanded no personal service
of her, and she could bear to spend the necessary time
at the far end of the Hall spinning or weaving. If she
were lucky, she'd be left alone and could think about
Kretheus. She was sure he was interested in her, and
she sang as she rummaged her chest to find her saffron-
dyed dress with the flounced skirt.

Nevertheless the hours in the presence of the Queen
dragged, and toward the end she left her loom and
walked restlessly about her end of the room, keeping an
eye on the chair near the light well, wondering if
Drupos would leave her, if she were late at the Guest
House where they were all to meet. When, released at
last by a nod from one of the Mycenean serving women,
she left the Hall quickly and went through the south
gate and crossed the ravine on the old arched bridge that
led to the Guest House, only one or two of the party

were there. Drupos was standing beside the Spring Chamber with its ever-filled lamp above the dark pool and its ledges for offerings to the Lady of the Fountains.

"Did you see any of the others, Thalamika?" he called as she came within earshot. She shook her head, still too breathless with hurrying to speak. He blew a few irritated and discordant notes upon the double-flute he was carrying.

"There's no hurry, cousin," she said, "they'll come. There's time enough. Philona was never one to make more haste than she has to. Look, there's Andrios on the bridge and the others aren't far behind him."

Drupos shouted Andrios' name and signed him to hurry, but Andrios came on at the same leisurely pace. Thalamika went a little way to meet him and ask his pardon away from Drupos. He gave it with good enough grace, though his eyes remained grave and he added, "You must have been overwrought, Thalamika, if you could see anything good in Kretheus. I'm sure he means us harm here in Crete, even though I can't see yet how he plans to accomplish it."

Thalamika could feel herself getting angry. There he was being pompous again, behaving as if he had the whole responsibility for the kingdom on his shoulders. But she didn't want to quarrel today and she said quickly, "Don't, Andrios. Past is past and today is for laughter."

He didn't smile but he said, "Very well, Thalamika. I'll not argue if you'll only give me your promise to avoid Kretheus and any of the men of Mycenae until I can find out more about their real intention at the Court of Minos."

Sing high, sing low,
So well we're met.
Let's sing our way
On journey set.

Spyros the Ever-Laughing saved Thalamika from answering. He capered up on the last words of his im-
promptu song, feet dancing, graceful arms spread wide.
In his black and white kilts he looked for all the world
like the mountain crow that soared and swooped above
his head.

Thalamika and Andrios joined the half-dozen young
men and women following him, and Thalamika managed
deftly to leave Andrios and walk with her friend Thalia,
who carried a lyre wreathed with a garland of asphodel
blossoms.

Drupos joined Spyros to lead the rest through the cool
pavilion of the Guest House, with its fresco of partridges
and hoopoes, and out again onto the great paved road to
the south.

The day was a perfection of gold and blue. Fields of
new green barley and millet shimmered in the sun haze
and the old gray-green olive trees—older than time,
twisted into a hundred weird shapes—marched up every
hillside. The high hills sprang above them, snow-
crowned, guardians of no man knew what ancient secrets.
Multicolored kilts and dresses were jewel-bright in the
clear air. The day and the land were made for joy, and
the gray, stooped field workers straightened their backs
and peered under their hands and bent again to their
hoes and mattocks the more willingly for the lighthearted
songs of the young ladies and gentlemen upon the road.

They had left Knossos five furlongs behind before
Drupos shouted and pointed, and they all saw what his
love-keen eyes had sensed rather than glimpsed. A dust
cloud marked the progress of a party of travelers.
Thalamika smiled. It might be nothing more than a merchant from the Land of the Pharaohs with his slaves and
retainers, coming with bales of fine linen cloth and
corn and alabaster and gold to trade at the Palace or in
the market at Amnisos for olive oil and honey and the
finest work of Cretan potters and jewelers. Or it might
be a messenger bringing the Priest-King a report on the
state of his realm. It might be a dozen ordinary people
going their ordinary ways, but Thalamika didn't believe
it. Not when she heard the gladness in Drupos' voice
and saw the light in his eyes. The Goddess Herself had
surely put into his mind the foreknowledge that his beloved Philona would emerge from the dust cloud.

He started to run, and Spyros would have run with
him if Thalamika hadn't laid a hand on his arm to stop
him. They waited and watched and saw a girl break from
the dust and come toward Drupos and into his arms
stretched out for her. Spyros shook off Thalamika's hand
and whooped a greeting and snatched Thalia's lyre and
went toward Drupos singing a courting song. Everyone
followed then and stood, while the cart carrying Philona's
belongings creaked up and stopped. Slaves, armed with
sharp bronze daggers, with bows and flint-tipped arrows
slung on their backs against the danger from brigands
in the mountains; and the Cretan woman who had been
Philona's nurse and companion since her mother's death
joined them and spread out across the road. The girls
surrounded Philona, asking questions, admiring her trav-

eling dress, touching her soft, loose blond hair, so different from their own dark formal curls. The young men teased Drupos, who couldn't decide whether to laugh or be angry at their jokes.

Thalamika stood a little apart, waiting for a chance to greet her friend properly. It was, she thought, strange how you forgot to notice differences in people you'd always known. Philona had come as a baby to Phaistos to be brought up by her uncle's wife. She and Thalamika had grown up together at the Palace Court, but it was now as if Thalamika were seeing for the first time that Philona's hair gave back to the sun the sun's own gold and that she wore it differently. She *is* half-Mycenean, Thalamika thought, and reared in Mycenean ways, though you'd go far to find anyone more loyal to Minos than Philona's uncle and aunt or, for that matter, Philona herself if she ever thought about politics.

Philona, looking over the heads of the strange new friends about her, caught Thalamika's eyes and sent her a look of appeal. Thalamika laughed and went toward the group. It was good to see Philona again, good to know they'd soon spend long hours of talk together. Only now did she realize how lonely she'd been in Knossos, in spite of all the people about her, in spite of new friends and entertainments and excitements. She could have cried for happiness as she put her hand on Philona's arm in greeting.

"Thank The Goddess you've come at last," Thalamika said. "I've missed you every hour of every day."

Philona tried to answer and stumbled over the words. Thalamika saw there were tears in her eyes and guessed she wasn't happy to be returning to her father's house.

"We'll talk later," Thalamika whispered, "it won't be too hard. You'll find new friends and new interests quickly enough, and we'll all help."

She squeezed Philona's arm and called out, "Come along, Drupos. It's time we went on or Philona's father will think we've turned into bandits and taken her into the high hills."

They made good time upon the return trip, leaving the cart and attendants well behind them. Thalamika watched Philona, frowning a little with worry. Philona was not like herself. She hardly said a word as she walked beside Drupos. She tried to smile at the jokes, but the smile wouldn't stay on her lips and she didn't join in the songs that one or another of the group started every time there was a pause in the talk. This home-coming, Thalamika thought, was more painful than she'd realized. And no wonder. Philona's father could be little more than a stranger to her. He hadn't come often to Phaistos during the sixteen years since he'd sent Philona there, and then only upon occasions of business when he'd been harried and hurried and had spent little time with his daughter.

Thalamika wished, not for the first time, that Drupos were a little more perceptive. She knew he adored Philona. But for him it was enough that he was beside her at last. He evidently took it for granted she was as content as he and didn't sense her unhappiness. Thalamika wondered what it was that bound the two so closely. Drupos, even though he was the very darling of all the young men and women of the Court, because he was easily the best boxer in all Crete, was a simple and direct person. And Philona, gay though she was most of the time, was subject to darker moods of doubt and misgivings about herself and the world about her. Thalamika decided she'd talk to Drupos and she'd plan to spend as much time as she could with Philona until her friend got accustomed to her new way of life.

In any case she had no more time to think about this problem just now, for they'd come again to the arched bridge beyond the Guest House. They circled about the Palace walls and went down the hill and through the center street of Amnisos to the roadway that led to the port. A small slave girl was sweeping the threshhold with a broom made of millet straw as they came to the House of Phelleus the Merchant. Seeing them come, the child dropped the broom and went inside the house hurriedly, closing the door behind her with a sharp smack. That's strange, Thalamika thought. Why would she close the door in the face of Phelleus' returning daughter? Maybe the little slave was newly come to house duties and didn't know any better. But Thalamika felt a curious pricking in her shoulder blades, which she recognized as a Goddess-sent warning of some evil thing about to happen.

Drupos drew a little away from Philona and stood forward, calling formally, "O Phelleus the Merchant, Chief of the Men of Mycenae in the country of Crete, come forth, for we have brought your daughter home with joy. We would come with her now into the house of her father and feast with you because she has come to live among us."

Silence. The shuttered windows, turning their blind eyes to the street, might well have marked the house of the newly dead. Drupos waited, expecting with each heartbeat to hear an answering call and a welcome.

When no one came to the house door he looked at his companions. They were as bewildered as he and he turned, as he always did when he was puzzled, to Andrios. "What should we do, Andrios?" he asked, but Andrios was as puzzled as he and shook his head. Thalamika put her arm around Philona, who stood rigidly, her eyes upon the ground, her face reddening for shame. Drupos waited a moment more, then called again, less courteously, "Ho! Phelleus, the Merchant, are you within?"

The door was thrust violently outward by a huge slave, who carried a heavy staff with which he barred the opening. His face, crossed from forehead to chin by an old scar, was sullen. He looked at the group before him and asked in a loud, harsh voice, "Which of you is Philona, daughter of Phelleus the Mycenean?"

Philona went forward until she stood clear of the others. She held herself very straight, and when she spoke her words came with a brittle sound of a stalactite breaking in the sacred cave on Mount Dichte.

"I am Philona, daughter of Andria, wife of Phelleus. Where *is* my father? He'll hear of this rude welcome to my friends."

The slave's ugly mouth opened in an ugly grin. Holding the staff with one hand, he reached the other toward Philona and would have taken her arm if Drupos and Spyros hadn't sprung forward and stood between the man and the girl, holding sharp daggers ready to strike. Drupos was too angry to speak, but Spyros spat at the slave's feet and said, "Take us at once to Phelleus so we can tell him how his slave greets his daughter."

Thalamika thought she saw a flicker of what seemed

to be amusement in the slave's eyes. His mouth twitched a little, or seemed to, as if he kept back a smile. She was puzzled for a moment before she decided she must have imagined the look of mirth. The slave stepped back into the doorway and spoke again from its shelter. "My master bids me tell you to leave the street before his house and stop troubling his peace with your noise. He sends word to all, but especially to Drupos the Boxer, that Philona is Mycenean and will choose no friends among the soft-minded and little men of Crete. He bids his daughter come in at once, to his hall where he waits to greet her with kindness and joy. If she doesn't come willingly and with speed, he says I'm to bring her by force even if it should be necessary to summon the Guardians of the Peace of the town."

Thalamika said, "You wouldn't dare. You . . ." but Philona, so white of face she seemed made of the snow that lay upon the high mountains, touched her arm and said, "No, Thalamika. This is not your cause. It is between me and my father. Go now. All of you go." She turned to the others and managed a half-smile that nearly broke Thalamika's heart. "Something's surely wrong here, and when it's been put right I'll ask you to come back to my father's house so he and I may explain and do you honor. But leave me now and—thank you all for your welcome." She turned again to Thalamika and said in a lower voice, "I'll get word to you and . . . and Drupos, Thalamika, as soon as I can."

She took a step toward the slave, not wavering at the look on his face. Thalamika wondered that she wasn't afraid until she saw that Philona had her hand upon the girdle of woven gold belting her loose, green dress, and that in the girdle was a dagger, the twin of Drupos'.

Before Philona could reach the door Drupos was beside her, holding her in his arms, saying something in her ear. Philona shook her head violently and the slave made a menacing noise, and Drupos dropped his arms and stepped back. Philona walked steadily toward the slave, and Thalamika let out her breath in relief as she saw him move aside. Philona passed, alone and spear-straight, into the house of her father.

They waited in silence until the slave followed her and the heavy door banged shut, then they started to chatter. But Drupos made a sign to Thalamika and Andrios and, without a word, turned his back upon his companions and started down the way that led to the shore. Thalamika and Andrios followed, and the three stood, watching the ordered confusion in the harbor, not speaking, for long minutes.

Drupos and Andrios had known Phelleus all their lives. They had known him as withdrawn and dour but as a man, if anything, overconscious of the opinion of his fellows and so carefully correct in his dealings with them that he sometimes appeared ridiculous. Thalamika had seen him when he came to Phaistos and he had treated her always with courtesy, though she had never felt he had any special kindness for her. What could have happened to cause a respected and successful merchant to turn his back upon the laws of hospitality? Even in the deserts of Nubia such conduct would bring censure from all decent-minded men. And Drupos. Why, Thalamika wondered, had Phelleus singled out Drupos to forbid him the house? Philona hadn't told anyone of their plans for marrying. How had her father known, for surely he must have known?

"How did he know about you and Philona, Drupos?" she asked, breaking the dam of silence that had held them. "He never saw you in Phaistos when you came visiting at our house and spent every hour with Philona. And Philona has told him nothing. I'd swear that upon the Horns of Consecration."

Drupos just looked at her, and Andrios gave a snort halfway between amusement and derision. "You talk with the voice of a child, Thalamika," he said, speaking more harshly than he'd intended because of his bewilderment. "There's no one in Knossos or Amnisos who doesn't know Philona is the beloved of Drupos the Boxer and expects to wed him at the next festival of the Spreading of the Couch. Drupos has been too happy to keep that counsel to himself."

She felt stupid and rebuked. Why must Andrios always be so superior, as if he knew all there was to know in the world, as if he thought everyone else were a fool? There wasn't any reason to make her feel an outcast because she hadn't known that gossip had been at work about Drupos and Philona.

He'd gone on speaking, and she'd missed something of what he'd said. His face was troubled and his voice carried a puzzled note. She was glad he wasn't sure of everything!

"A man may bar his own door against those he would keep without. Even in Crete. Even so near the House of the Priest-King, where all who came in peace are welcome at all times. And yet, I don't like it. Why should Phelleus, who's lived most of his life among us, who

chose his wife from among us, and is honored by the
Priest-King himself as leader of the foreign merchants;
why should he forbid his daughter to choose Cretan
friends? Especially now with a Mycenean embassy just
come to ask for better trading conditions? I don't understand it and I don't like it. Kretheus . . ."

Drupos whirled from staring out to sea and shouted at
him. "You, Andrios! Why do you go on asking questions
you can't answer while my Philona's being held prisoner
by that . . . that . . . wild bull of a man? He may do
her harm. We must save her. We must . . ."

"Drupos!" Andrios said peremptorily. "Think what
you're saying. It isn't likely that Phelleus will harm his
only daughter, except perhaps in her pride, and . . ."

"Not *Phelleus*, Andrios. The slave," Drupos shouted.

"Oh, the slave," Andrios said and smiled. "Don't worry
about the slave. I've known him for as long as I can remember. He used to carry me on his shoulders through
the market place at Amnisos, when I was not much big-
ger than a grasshopper. He's quite harmless. He was once,
before he was taken in a pirate raid and sold as a slave,
famous as an actor in Troy. It amuses him now and then
to practice his art upon the unsuspecting, though I must
say I thought his miming ill-timed today. But I don't
blame him. It's only when he's acting that he can forget
he's a slave. He has a gentle heart. He won't harm your
Philona."

So, Thalamika thought, she'd been right about the
slave's hidden laughter.

"Just the same we must rescue her," Drupos said, but
Andrios shook his head.

"No, Drupos," he said. "It would be unlawful. Philona

isn't yet of an age where she can defy her father's authority, even by the laws of Crete. You would only be seized by the Guardians of the Peace and, if Phelleus chose, lashed. There's nothing we can do. Nothing except wait for Phelleus to get over his crazy whim."

Drupos took a step toward Andrios and faced him. "Unlawful, Andrios? What's your law to me when Philona is taken from me? When I'm told not to see her or talk to her? If you won't help me, leave me so you won't be smirched by my unlawfulness. For I'm going to help her."

Andrios looked as surprised as if Drupos had struck him in the face, and Thalamika said, "Be quiet, Drupos! You're too upset to know what you're saying. Would you put Philona into real danger by your foolish actions? And you, Andrios! You see the shadow of danger behind every bush. It's you two who are thinking with the minds of children now. Until we hear some word from Philona, we can't know the truth of what's happening. I know her better than either of you. Yes, Drupos, even better than you. She promised to get word to us. She'll do it somehow. So we'd better leave off this aimless talk and speculation and go home where she can find us if she wants us."

CHAPTER
FIVE

Drupos stubbornly refused to leave the harbor town. He raved against Phelleus until Thalamika began to fear he was demon-haunted. But Andrios saw reason in her argument and gradually calmed Drupos until, at last, they took the long hill-way back to the Palace, wordless because Drupos wouldn't say anything and his deep-shadowing silence forbade talk. As they came over the last slope Andrios whispered to her to go on ahead, for he planned to take Drupos to the Exercise Field and get him to rid himself of his anger and hurt in practicing for the sports demonstration planned to entertain the Myceneans.

Thalamika went straight to her aunt's house, hoping to find a message waiting. There was none and she wandered aimlessly about for an hour, hoping for some word from Philona. When still none came, she decided to go back to Amnisos.

She hurried toward the market place with its stalls shaded by gay awnings of blue and red, striped with white, brave in the glowing day. Maybe, in this place where all the world seemed to meet to bargain in trade and hear the latest news, she might get some word of her friend.

Usually she delighted to walk among the stalls. But today the sunburned sailors from Spain and Egypt; black-skinned men from Nubia; dark-bearded Hittites with their sloping foreheads and long, aquiline noses; fair-faced Myceneans with short, blond beards only irritated her as they jostled for place before the booths of cloth merchants, jewelers, food sellers, and potters with their beautiful ceramic cups and vases and lamps. The sky-rising babble of words in a dozen tongues had no power to please her ears. She twisted and turned among the narrow, stone-paved streets, listening for the name of Philona or Phelleus. She was about to give up her search when she heard, or thought she heard, her own name whispered and followed the sound into a narrow opening between a stone house and a wooden stall and felt arms about her and heard Philona's voice.

"Praise Zeus and Apollo you've come, Thalamika. I couldn't send you a message because no one would take it for me today, so I've waited here the gods know how long hoping you'd come."

The narrow way was shade-drenched, and Philona showed as little more than a darker silhouette in the shadows. But Thalamika could guess her distress by her tense voice and trembling hands.

"I'm here, Philona," Thalamika said, pouring as much encouragement as she could into the words. "Now tell me."

"I think Phelleus, my father, is god-cursed to madness, Thalamika," Philona said in a rush. Thalamika started to interrupt, but Philona went on. "No. Hear me out." Thalamika was quiet, leaning against the house wall, listening.

"You know my grandfather brought my father here from the Argolis when he was a small boy. My father grew up here with the people of the Priest-King and took them for his own people, and my father and grandfather kept the ways and customs of Crete, for my father's father was a wise man. He hoped to spend his whole lifetime here and prosper as a merchant in the land of Minos, and he wanted to live as the Cretans lived. It was only in our house shrine that he kept to his own customs and worshiped the Mycenean gods, though he held your Goddess always in respect."

"I know all these things, Philona," Thalamika said, a little impatiently. "Must you . . . ?"

"Yes, Thalamika, I must, for it's only in this way that I can make everything clear to myself as well as to you. My grandfather died when my father had just come to manhood. My aunt had married another merchant from Mycenae and gone with him to Phaistos, where he managed my father's concerns in the south. Father took command of the business here and increased the fleet of trading ships and prospered. And when the next month of the Spreading of the Couch came, he married Andria, my mother, who was a Cretan lady. He loved her deeply, but at my birth she died and the women who attended her said the cause of her death was my father's failure to make the proper offerings to your Goddess in her cave shrine at Eileithyia."

Philona had been speaking faster and faster. Thalamika could hardly understand her, and she said, "Wait a little, Philona. Take a breath and rest, or you'll do yourself harm."

"I'm all right, Thalamika. Please listen carefully because there's something you must do for me. Tell Drupos what's happened to me and tell him not to worry and warn Andrios, though I don't exactly know against what."

She did pause then and took three shuddering breaths, while Thalamika stroked the soft, yellow hair that marked her Mycenean ancestry. When she went on, Philona was a little calmer.

"It was then, Thalamika, my father turned against all things and all the people of this country. If your Goddess could visit her disfavor upon the guiltless and make my mother a shade, he swore by all his gods he would hate the land and the people who honored such a deity all his days and find ways to harm them."

Thalamika made the sign against evil, shocked by such blasphemy against The Goddess, but Philona didn't notice the small gesture and went on. "He vowed that day my mother died I should be reared in the way of Mycenae and when I was a year old sent me with my nurse to my aunt in Phaistos, thinking she would teach me the customs of her home and his." She laughed a little but there was no humor in the sound. "My father didn't trouble to come to see us often, and when he came he asked no questions. He was stiff-necked and arrogant, and he felt no need to search his sister's heart. So he had no shadow of doubt that she and her husband had abandoned most of the ancient ways of his people and become, as you know them, like the people of Crete. So my father thought I, too, was a Crete-hater until he began to hear talk of my love for Drupos and this made him suspicious and he sent for me. When he saw me brought to the door with singing and joy, he flew in anger and now, *now*, Thalamika, he swears he'll keep me house-bound, watched and guarded as a common thief, until I promise to forget my friends and deny this laughing land that is half mine by birth and all mine by love. But I won't do it. I—will—*not*. I cannot."

As she finished the sun in its sky coursing moved into the space between the house and the stall and sent a shaft of brilliant light into the doorway. A small, white butterfly flew into the light and hovered over Philona's head. Thalamika, watching it, spoke softly. "See, Philona. Even as you speak of her, your mother's soul comes to bring you courage."

"My mother's soul?" Philona asked wonderingly.

"See. The white butterfly. Have you forgotten what I told you about our belief that the souls of shades come back to their loved ones as butterflies? She's near you, Philona. She'll help us think what to do."

"What *can* I do, Thalamika? It isn't likely I'll have another chance to steal away from the house. My father's bound to hear how I tricked the woman left to watch me into getting me a cure for headache and so got out. He'll surely double my guard."

"Make a pretense of submitting so you'll be free," Thalamika suggested.

"I will not deny my mother's land and her people. Not even in pretense." Philona's eyes were on the butterfly still fluttering in the sun's shaft. For a second it lit on the blue band that bound her hair, then flew away.

Philona sighed and said, "Besides, Thalamika, it wouldn't do any good to pretend submission to his will. He believes he can bring me to do what he wants if he keeps me prisoner long enough and talks to me enough about Mycenae. He says as soon as I come to my senses and obey him he'll send me straightway to King Lyssus. So even if I did pretend, it would only mean I'd be sent away from Crete and you and—Drupos forever."

"By the Labrys," Thalamika said, "Phelleus must be mad. I can't see anything for you to do, then, except stand fast against him until we can free you, Drupos and I and"—she found herself adding almost against her will —"Andrios. But we'd better make a plan to keep in touch with each other. Is there anyone you can trust, someone free to come and go from the House of Phelleus?"

"My nurse. She's afraid of my father, but I think her love for me is greater than any fear."

"Good. Then each seventh day at this same time send her here. I'll be waiting or Drupos or Andrios. And . . ." she pulled at her lower lip, thinking, "and if you need us urgently between times, hood your lamp with a red cloth just after darkfall and I'll have Chryses watch each night and tell me, and one of us will come here next day for your message."

Philona nodded agreement and put her arms word-lessly around Thalamika, before she started toward the end of the alleyway that led from the market place. But she took only three steps before she came back and called to Thalamika, who, in her turn, was moving slowly in the other direction.

"Wait, Thalamika! I forgot the warning for Andrios. Tell him—tell him I'm certain Phelleus, my father, plots some evil thing against the Priest-King."

"What kind of evil thing, Philona?" Thalamika asked as she came back to the center of the alley.

"I don't know anything certain, Thalamika. But my room's above my father's work chamber and the floor be-

tween is thin. While I waited this morning I heard many
men come—by stealth, for they didn't call the gatekeeper
to open the house door. They talked with my father in
the language of the Myceneans. I couldn't hear everything. They kept their voices low. But someone said,
quite clearly, 'When Minos is gone,' and another spoke
a name, 'Kretheus.'"

Thalamika said, sharply, "Kretheus! What . . ."

"Do you know the name, Thalamika? I hadn't heard
it before. Who is this Kretheus?"

"He's head of an embassy from King Lyssus to Minos.
It's only something to do with trade, Philona. There
couldn't be any harm in it."

"Well, I'm only telling you what I heard. I'm afraid my
father and his friends are planning some mischief against
the Priest-King, and I think someone should be warned."

Thalamika thought Philona was so upset by all that
had happened she was imagining danger where none
existed. Still, it would probably be better to humor her.
It couldn't do any harm to tell Drupos, and he could take
the story to Andrios if he wished. The name of
Kretheus could be kept out of it.

"I'll tell Drupos what you've told me, Philona," Thalamika said. "But you'd better go now. It wouldn't be
good for Phelleus or one of his slaves to find us here together, and you've been away long enough to be missed.
Your father may already have sent someone to look for
you. Don't forget our plans for keeping in touch with
each other."

Thalamika found Drupos waiting outside the door of
his father's house. He was pacing the steep street, his
back straight as one of the Palace Guard's, his face set in

a frown. She could tell, even from a distance, that the hours of hard exercise had helped. It was obvious that Drupos had rid himself of the worst of his anger and was ready to think more sensibly. He called, when she was near enough to hear, "Did you see her, Thalamika?" and when Thalamika nodded he ran to meet her and took her arm and shook it a little. "Tell me! Quickly!"

"Not here, Drupos. There'll be curious people passing." He started impatiently toward the house door, and she said, "Nor in the house. Slaves have ears and a deal of curiosity. What I've got to tell you must be kept secret. Come to the Sacred Way and let's walk along toward the House of the Priestess. There's not likely to be anybody there this time of day."

"But, Thalamika, I must *know* and it'll take time to go to the Sacred Way. I can't wait so long. Tell me now."

"Do you want to bring danger to her, Drupos?" As usual Thalamika found herself impatient with Drupos for wanting to act first and think later. "Do as I say and make light talk as we go along. And stop looking as dark as a rain cloud on Mount Dichte. Pretend you're teasing me. Laugh, no matter how shadowed your heart may be. Come on."

She led him, walking steadily but not too quickly around the Palace and toward the grove of pine trees whispering together in the light breeze from the sea. He did as she said and set his face in a show of his usual good humor. When the pines hid them from the thousand eyes of the Palace, they quickened their walk and came to the paved way bordered on each side with dark, straight yew trees that led from the dancing place to the

House of the Priestess, a quarter hour's walk from the House of the Priest-King. When they had gone half the distance and made sure no one was about to overhear them, she told him of her meeting with Philona.

He heard her out and when she was done stood in the road, his mind working slowly over what she'd said. "It's well," he said at last. "Or rather it's all we can do now. She's likely safe enough. I'll talk to Andrios and maybe, between us, we can think of some way to rescue my love from that—that madman."

"What of her fears for Minos, Drupos? Do you believe them?"

He pulled at his lip as she had done earlier, as her mother and his did when they searched their minds. When he spoke, it was carefully as if he had to puzzle out each word. "It's not like Philona to imagine things," he said. "In all the time I've known her since I saw her first when I came as a little boy to stay with your mother, Philona has never been one to deal in imaginings. And yet, it doesn't seem reasonable that Phelleus—Poseidon sink his ships!—would plot against us. He's chief of all the merchants in Amnisos, and without the strong Cretan fleet the seas would still be pirate-scourged. Why would a man plot to ruin his own business? Though he hates us and all Crete, he wouldn't destroy himself with it. And yet—if Philona says he means us mischief . . ." He shook his head. He found so much thinking tiresome. "You'd better tell Andrios. He'll know what to do. He's close to the counsels of Minos. He's gone half a day's journey toward the west to inspect a guard post, but he'll surely be at the sports tomorrow. Watch for him and tell him privately what you've told me."

CHAPTER
SIX

Thalamika almost forgot her dignity and skipped like a small girl as she followed the bull team on its way to capture wild bulls for the festival of The Goddess and Her Consort Poseidon. Kretheus, the Mycenean, walked beside her, holding her hand lightly in his, swinging their two hands in time to the gay tune Spyros was improvising upon his flute. She thought she'd never been so happy in all her life. The week since the sports had been as full and overflowing with happiness as a libation cup ready to be spilled for The Lady.

She had seen Kretheus—really seen him to talk to—first at the end of the demonstration of the athletes. She'd sat, with the other young Priestesses, just behind him in the stands along the sides of the Central Court and had forgotten the wrestlers; forgotten even the Egyptian tumblers, the men supporting their skyward-turned bodies upon their hands or elbows, the women with hands or feet firmly upon the ground, arching their bodies backward into a perfect bow. All this was old and familiar and not nearly so fascinating as the bright, cropped curls of the man in front of her. Then the boxers, led by Drupos, carrying their gloves, their hands and wrists wound in the leather bands of the cestus to protect their muscles from strain, marched into the Court. She turned her mind from Kretheus and rose to her feet as everyone else in the stands rose, shouting delight in the boxers who, after the bull leapers, held first place in the hearts of all Cretans.

She shouted with the rest, and her sweet, clear voice was plainly distinguished in the roar as she called her special greetings to Drupos. He, hearing her as the boxers halted and faced the Myceneans, lifted his gloves to her. Then Kretheus had turned full around to see who was so honored by the chief of the boxers and smiled into her face and saluted her. He was so close she could see the circle of tiny red dots tattooed lightly into the skin of his cheekbones and smell the perfumed oil upon his body beneath the purple tunic that marked him a Prince of Mycenae.

She could not—or would not—look anywhere except into his eyes. They were gray or blue or green—sometimes one, sometimes another, depending upon the light and the quick-changing expressions that followed his nimble thoughts. The eyes glittered as, she imagined from traveler's tales she'd heard, the eyes of the basilisk glittered. They stood thus while the crowd roared and the broad-shouldered, narrow-waisted, strong-muscled boxers lifted their arms in acceptance of the shouts; while the shouting died away and the crowd sat down until only the two of them were still upon their feet.

Laughter, running along the rows of cushion-covered wooden benches, and a twitch at her elbow released Thalamika from the spell of Kretheus' eyes. She dropped down quickly, with a little thump, and he bowed toward her, no bit embarrassed, and said clearly and with the proper formality, "Will you honor me, O Thalamika the Beautiful, by dining in my quarters this day?" He waited for her nod of acceptance—for she was too confused to speak—then he, too, took his seat.

The exhibition of boxing was almost over before she could quiet her disjointed thoughts and give her attention to the skill of the men in the Court below. Drupos, to no one's surprise, was named winner and had been crowned with a garland of yellow crocus blossoms, and the crowd was shouting its pleasure and approval again, when she remembered she'd promised to warn Andrios of Philona's fears for the Priest-King. She looked for him in his usual place before the entrance to the Audience Room but, though the section of seats reserved for the King's special servants was nearly full, Andrios wasn't there, and she shrugged and forgot him.

She hadn't seen Andrios in all the week since. When she asked Drupos where he was, he had no information. It was evident Andrios had changed his plans. Probably the Priest-King, Drupos had said, had sent Andrios to check with the tax-gatherers at the far end of the island. There'd been rumors of anger among the people at the size of this year's levy; rumors of grain and olives withheld and hidden, and collectors set upon with stones. Andrios knew how to humor the farmers and small artisans and he would be the natural choice for dealing with such problems. She and Drupos had agreed the delay wouldn't matter. Especially, since, when Thalamika had gone yesterday to talk with Philona's nurse, there'd been no further word of plots and fears. Philona was restless and unhappy in the house where, as she had expected, the guards upon the house doors had been doubled, and Drupos, though he tried to drive his mind to plans, hadn't as yet thought of a way to trick Phelleus into releasing his daughter.

The memory of these things and of the hours each day when she had met Kretheus secretly, because he wished their meetings to be secret, ran with Spyros' tune through Thalamika's head. She'd been surprised this morning when Kretheus had openly sought her outside the Court of the Bull Leapers. She'd gone there early to wait the beginning of the annual walk to a defile in the mountains, where wild bulls, lured from their well-watered pastures on Mount Ida by the mournful cries of a decoy cow, could be captured. All the members of the Mycenean embassy had been invited to go with the bull team and watch the sport, and as usual every young Cretan at the Palace had come along to cheer on the leapers, who would attempt to fill the bull pens beneath the Palace with prize animals fit to honor The Lady and Poseidon at the Bull Games, which would follow the harvest.

Thalamika, as she came early to the Bull Leapers' Court, reviewed her latest audience with the Woman of Mycenae. Myrtis had sent for her only the day before and, when she stood with eyes lowered in a pretense of humility, had hissed like an angry house snake, "Why do you defy my orders, girl?"

Thalamika had looked up, genuinely surprised, and said, "I don't understand, O Myrtis, Queen of Crete. I haven't disobeyed an order of yours."

The Queen smiled in a nasty way and spoke sarcastically. "Ah, then. So you are living, as I bade you, in the Court of the Bull Leapers, sharing their hard beds and eating their coarse food!" She looked at the benches in the long hall filled with her handmaidens bidden to come here to witness Thalamika's discomfiture before she roared, "NO, Thalamika of Phaistos! Do not try to lie to me, for I know the truth. You have *not* left your uncle's home. You have *not* obeyed my orders. You thought you could fool me but I have my own spies and I know. WELL! Speak. Answer me."

"If it pleases the Queen," Thalamika had said, and the very calmness of her voice seemed to mock the angry woman before her, "I did as the Queen bade me and went to the Court of the Bull Leapers with the Queen's order on my tongue. But the Guardian of the Court sent me away, saying that no one was permitted within the Court while the leapers were training for the Bull Games."

She would have gone on, but the Queen's face had turned white and she had shouted down the length of the hall asking if this were true. And when the handmaidens had, as one person, answered "Yes," Myrtis, shaking and barely coherent, had ordered Thalamika from her sight and banned her from the Queen's Hall during the Queen's pleasure.

Silly old fool, Thalamika was thinking to herself with a grin as Kretheus came up behind her softly and put his hands under her elbows and lifted her off her feet. She'd known at once it was he, for her nerves jumped to his touch and the blood ran more quickly in her veins.

"Hail, Thalamika," he said, putting her down none too gently, for he was full of energy and a gaiety she hadn't seen in him before. "Spyros says that today each man chooses his own companion to walk beside him to the

bull capturing, and I've chosen you, for you are the love-
liest of all the ladies I've seen in this island of Crete.
You'll stay beside me the whole day and explain the
meaning of your customs, and I'll bring you home in joy
when evening comes."

For a moment she felt only anger at him. He didn't ask
but commanded, and she wasn't used to commands. But
her anger was quickly stilled by a rush of happiness because he'd chosen her. She said to him teasingly, "What's
happened to your secrecy, Kretheus, Prince of Mycenae?"

He laughed at her, bending down a little to see into
her face. "The time for hiding is over and past, Thalamika. It may take some men months to make up their
minds, but a week's enough for me and so . . ." He left
the sentence dangling, and she thought is he telling me
a week's enough for him to know his love, and answered
yes to her own question and would have put her hands
upon his and declared her growing delight in him, had
not Spyros' laughter run before him to warn her that others
were coming.

Many others did come quickly, to join the three waiting for the great wooden doors to open to the bull team.
The crowd was restless, eager to start the hour's journey
to the defile. They shifted their places and called from
group to group, laughing and laying wagers on the number of bulls that would be taken. Two of the girls had
brought along a gaming board, beautifully inlaid with
rock crystal. They opened it and set it between them on
a stone bench against the wall and began to snap thin
ivory counters, painted in gaudy colors, into two small
golden cups.

Kretheus leaned against the cool stones of the Palace

wall and looked about him. He was very still, and Thalamika as she watched him thought he'd forgotten her
and wondered what was in his mind. His eyes were
hooded under his long lashes and told her nothing, but
she sensed in him some sudden withdrawal from the
friendly talk around him. There was something tense
about him and brooding that contrasted strangely with
his good humor of a moment before. She was a little
frightened by the change in him. She wanted to speak
to him but she didn't dare. She thought he might be
communing with his own gods and she wouldn't in that
case disturb him.

He wasn't conscious that she was looking at him. He
was, suddenly, sick for his homeland across the Great
Green Sea; sick for his own people, spear carriers, lovers
of war and the chase, who would disdain the soft luxury
of this rich island, where singing and dancing took the
place of the sterner disciplines of mind and body that
made a nation strong. He was tired of rich food and soft
beds and the endless color of pictured walls and golden
vessels and elaborately decorated pottery. He was pic-
turing himself upon his own stark hilltop, among men
who talked of war not flowers, and women who seldom
left their own quarters and knew their proper place in a
world of men. His hands ached for the feel of shield
and spear as his mind ached for the tough, barrack-room
talk of men. When would his work here be over? He
hadn't thought it would take so long, but nobody hurried
in this land of peace-lovers steeped in luxury. Even the
Mycenean merchants had been affected and would do
nothing in a rush. When could he go back to Mycenae
and hear his King and Lord call the work well done?

Beside him Thalamika drew a little away from him, and the slight swish of her dress was enough to rouse him from his thoughts. He blinked his eyelids once, owl-like, and looked at her and smiled and she forgot her doubts and uncertainties.

"Why are we waiting?" he asked. "Why don't we get about this bull capturing?"

"Probably the Bull Master is choosing who'll be net-men and who leapers. It always takes time. Every bull leaper wants to help capture the first wild bulls of the year, and it's sometimes hard to choose among all the boys and girls."

"Girls?" Kretheus' eyes opened wide and his voice was unbelieving. "Surely women don't take part in such dangerous sport as bull capturing!"

"Why not? They're as quick and lithe as the boys and as brave."

"In my country, our girls are not so forward." His voice was disapproving now, and she thought she'd better switch his mind to something else. "Tell me of your country," she said.

"My country." He looked at her with a faraway, lonely look, and she thought he's homesick for his own land. "How can I make you see my country, Thalamika?" His speech had become rhythmic and sonorous like the speech of the bards. "My country is a great fertile plain full of green vines and waving seas of millet and barley and, on the gray guardian hills, many olive groves. In the midst of the plain rises a great rock and, upon its top, a mighty fortress whose walls are made of stones so thick and strong no enemy can cast them down. It's said the Cyclops themselves threw up the wall in some bygone day, but to that I cannot witness. The wall is pierced by one gate, and high above it, growing as it seems from the very hilltop, is a citadel whose windows look out and out across the plain to the blue, clear waters of the bay named Argos, where our warships and our merchant ships crowd the beaches the year long. And daylong and nightlong the walls are watched and guarded by strong-limbed men-at-arms, whose far-reaching spears are thirsty for the blood of our enemies."

He stopped and she waited, thinking he would go on but his eyes looked inward again—or outward upon some vision she couldn't see.

"Do you," she asked in wonder, "in your country think always of war and enemies? Don't you sometimes laugh and turn your minds to the making of beautiful things as we do here? Don't you ever dance and make music and delight in the gifts of the"—she had been about to say "of The Goddess" and remembered the strange multitude of Mycenean gods and changed the words—"of the fair earth?"

"Such things are for weaklings," he said roughly, as if he were angry with her. "We've no time in Mycenae for dabbling with clay nor yet for painting walls. If we want such things, we send out ships for them or for the men to make them for us. Myceneans are not soft as . . ."

"They're coming!" It was Spyros, more keen-eared than the rest, who gave the cry and a second later the huge gates of the Bull Leapers' Court were opened and a dozen boys and girls came through in double file. The crowd drew apart to give them room and, after the first cry of "Hail!" fell silent while the bull leapers raised their arms in unison and lifted their voices to invoke

The Goddess and beg good fortune from her. Then the gates closed, creaking a little on heavy bronze hinges, and the leapers broke rank and mingled with the crowd, greeting special friends and giving news of other favorites training in the Court.

Thalamika didn't take part in the confused moment. She had no special friends among the chosen twelve, and she was uncertain and troubled by Kretheus' unfinished sentence. Had he been about to add "Cretans" to his scornful and angry comparison? Did he hate this land and its people as his voice suggested? Then why had he been sent to cajole better terms from Minos? She thought he'd been so carried away by his own remembering he'd forgotten where he was or whom he was with, and she wondered, fleetingly, if Andrios could be right about him. She wanted to look up into his face, but she was afraid of what it might tell her. It was just then, when she'd been carefully not looking at him, he'd taken her hand and squeezed it a little and said, "Why are we standing here, Thalamika? Look, the bull capturers are on their way. Let's follow them."

They'd run together, hand in hand, until they came up to the others and followed closely, talking lightly of the warm spring day and the flowers, blue and mauve, pink and white and golden yellow, that starred the ground beneath the dusky green olive groves and mantled the steep-sloping hillsides. Rather, she had talked and he had listened, or seemed to, watching her face change with her thoughts, forgetting how much he disliked the forward Cretan women in admiration of her flashing beauty.

They heard the call of the tethered cow and a far-answering roar from the mountain while they were still minutes away from the defile and once again those who had come to watch drew away from the bull capturers. Kastor, leader of the team, spoke quietly, telling them all to keep downwind of the defile so they wouldn't warn the keen-nosed bulls; telling them to take their watching stations softly and remain silent. Then he, with the other bull leapers, went straight on toward the defile, and the rest climbed the mountainside and found places where they could see the decoy cow.

Thalamika pulled Kretheus down behind an outcropping boulder, warning him with finger to lip against talk. He whispered, his mouth close against her ear, "Have no fear for me, my lovely. I, too, have captured bulls for Poseidon." She nodded, remembering that all the peoples living about the Great Green Sea also honored the Bull Tamer with sacrifice of his most worthy creatures. Another great bull roar, nearer than before, echoed from the high hills and another and another and a rush of sound that was almost tangible drowned her answering whisper.

The bull team had come to the opening of the defile, and the members were separating, each going quietly and quickly to his appointed task. One of the boys climbed the steep sides of the hill, his slight, lithe body seeming to go straight up as if he were in truth a creature of the rock. The others worked quickly, spreading the net they had brought across the mouth of the defile, anchoring it with strong rope deftly threaded through bronze rings set in the rock face. The decoy cow spoke mournfully and the bull answered, very close now. Then the mighty creature came cautiously into their viewline, and Thalamika caught her breath.

He was, indeed, a bull fit for Poseidon, all white except for a rim of black about one eye and a black tip to his tail. He was so big he seemed to dwarf the steep rocks over which he picked his steps on hoofs as dainty as a goat's. He stopped where the defile opened and swung his great head from side to side, snuffling the light air, as if he would smell out any danger. He stood so, poised, watchful while all the hidden spectators counted their heartbeats. The cow lowed again, and the fierce, beautiful animal above her trumpeted an answer and started his precipitous run down the defile toward the mild-eyed heifer he would take for his mate.

He saw the spreading net too late and too late checked his mighty stride. The heavy rope, cross-woven, tangled his hoofs and before he could free them the bull leaper hidden above, soaring from the high rocks like some giant man-bird, was upon his back, grappling his horns to the ground; forcing, slight-bodied skill against mindless strength, the mighty shoulders to the ground.

The bull thrashed and struggled, but the will of his antagonist drove him deeper into the tangling meshes until the heart went out of him and he lay quietly at last, unhurt except in his pride. The bull team worked quickly then, for already another roaring announced another comer from the pastures. They freed hoofs and horns and withdrew the net and prodded the beaten animal, too mazed for the moment and frightened to resist, to its feet. One of the boys, keeping his eyes always upon the animal's legs lest it strike out against its enemy, slipped a heavy rope noose about a fetlock and tethered the white bull near the cow.

The capturers hid themselves again. The bull waited,

trembling, hearing above him the call of a rival, yet fearful still of danger from the unknown creature that had trapped him. No sound, no shifting air, brought danger signs to his tight, small ears or wide-opened nostrils. The trembling in him lessened, ceased. He turned his head and nosed the cow curiously.

CHAPTER
SEVEN

Thalamika moved carefully to get into a more comfortable position behind the screening rock. She was bored, and tired of watching the bull capturers going, methodically now, about their business. After the netting of the white leader, the capture of late-coming bulls had been unexciting.

They came singly, as if each would give the other a chance. And they came slowly, not magnificently rushing as the first had come. Each seemed almost to tiptoe down the defile toward the tethered animals, peering ahead as if trying to understand why the cow and the white bull stood so quietly. And as each appeared, the capturers came out of their hiding places and caught the new, puzzled arrival by the horns and threw him and hobbled his legs so quickly he had no time to fight, then led him off and hid him away from the defile. It was a brave sight and the skill of the team was, at first, a delight to watch. But after a time it became monotonous.

Thalamika looked at Kretheus, wishing they could talk, and found him stretched upon his back, asleep. She was affronted, but she reminded herself quickly that she, too, was bored. She watched him for a while and began to feel tenderness for the big, relaxed body and wondered that he could sleep so soundly this early in the day. She shifted her own position once more so she shaded his face from the sun, and watched a pair of mountain crows dip and soar down toward the mountain rocks and up again straight, it seemed to her, at the sun while bull after bull came from the high pastures and was taken.

She, too, was almost asleep, lulled into a half-trance by sun and stillness and the nearness of Kretheus, when Kastor raised the cry that put an end to the day's sport. Kretheus didn't stir and when, finally, she succeeded in waking him he was cross and slow to start down the mountain. Why couldn't she leave him alone, he thought. He'd been up till dawn last night on business for his King, and he was tired. He followed her sulkily.

They came into the road that ran toward Knossos as a goatboy drove his flock across it. The black animals straggled aimlessly. The boy ran at them, making little jabbing thrusts with his thonged stick at one or another, trying to herd them toward the mountainside. When, at last, he had them across the road and bounding up the steep slopes toward fresh forage, the way toward Knossos was empty; the company that had come to watch the bulls disappeared around a bend. But, from the other direction, a dust cloud rolled toward Kretheus and Thalamika and resolved itself into three men on she-asses, ambling along the road.

One of the men prodded his animal into a reluctant run and, when he was still a little distance away, called out, "Hola! Thalamika. Well met."

Kretheus had already started striding toward Knossos,

paying no attention to Thalamika, leaving her to follow behind him. He turned at the shout and shaded his eyes against the sun and stared at the man as dusty as the beast he rode. The stranger's hair was disarranged and, even from this distance, it was easy to see a dark line that marked the stubble of unplucked beard upon his chin. He looked a peasant, and Kretheus' crossness flared into ill-temper that such a lout should dare hail a lady in the company of a Prince of Mycenae. For that matter, he thought, disgust at Thalamika's free and easy ways with him overcoming the spell of her beauty, no lady of Mycenae would *be* alone with him upon the road. Nevertheless, here it was the custom and he would teach the rude fellow a lesson he'd not soon forget. Yet, some deep-seated caution warned him against haste and he stayed where he was and shouted back along the way, "Who *is* that man, Thalamika?"

Thalamika knew, had known from his first word, that it was Andrios who called to her. But she was angry with Kretheus. He'd treated her shamefully when he strode away from her, leaving her to run after him if she wanted to go back to Knossos in his company. She would now treat unmannerliness with discourtesy, and she didn't turn toward Kretheus or answer him but walked forward to meet Andrios.

He got down stiffly from the ass and she saw he was tired. His face was pale beneath the dust in spite of the sun-deep tan of his skin. His eyes were dark-circled as if he hadn't slept much, but he looked at her gladly and stretched out his hands to her, and again she sensed that surprising laughter in him and was glad for it.

"How many bulls, Thalamika?" he asked. "I wanted

to be your partner today, but"—his eyes clouded with worry—"there's trouble among the people in the West, and Minos sent me . . ."

He got no further. Kretheus, angry as one of the wild bulls, set Thalamika roughly aside and stood in her place, glowering down upon Andrios, who stood in his riding cloak a full head shorter than he.

"What is the meaning of this shameful address to my lady?" Kretheus said, voice tight and harsh. He still didn't recognize Andrios beneath the road dust. "Are Cretan peasants taught no manners? Or don't you know the difference between a yokel and a lady of the Court? It's not so in *my* country."

"*Your* lady, Kretheus?" Andrios spoke mildly, but the look upon his face wasn't mild. "Thalamika, daughter of Kalmia of Phaistos, is, I think, no man's lady—as yet."

"You would call me a liar, little man?" Kretheus roared at him. "Look at me! I am Kretheus, Prince of Mycenae, and I could break your back with my hands and will, once I know your name."

"I think not, Kretheus of Mycenae. Indeed you should know better than to make such a boast having already felt the strength of my arms. Mind your words, *Prince* Kretheus. No man threatens Andrios of Knossos unless he would live to regret his threat."

Kretheus had raised his hands, widespread, groping, and shortened the space between them by a step. Andrios gave no ground, and Thalamika remembered that he, too, was a prince though he was slow to claim it— prince and nephew of Minos the Priest-King; Cupbearer and Lord of Knossos. And, she thought, at this moment, in spite of dirt and road grime, unplucked beard, and

sleep-needing eyes, he looked every cubit of his titles.
She remembered, too, he had been counted best of all
the bull leapers in the memory of living men, and she
knew she wanted no fight between these two for her sake.
She called out sharply, "No!" but her warning was not
needed. Kretheus had dropped his threatening hands
slowly and moved a little away from Andrios. "If you'd
named yourself at once, Andrios of Knossos, you could
have saved us both unpleasantness. I took you for some
farm laborer."

Andrios looked at him, not bothering to answer the
half-apology. The more he saw of this Mycenean, the less
he liked or trusted him. Thalamika, still bitter at Kretheus' churlishness, felt a warm and quick affection and
pride for Andrios. Why, she thought, I really do *like*
him. He might be plodding and far too serious, but he
was a Prince of Crete and his courage was many spans
higher than his stature. She started to go to him in friendship, but he spoke to her sharply, not taking his eyes off
Kretheus, and his peremptory words were blows upon her
new-found affection.

"Mount the ass, Thalamika," he ordered. "I'll take you
home to your aunt. Didn't I warn you against Kretheus?
Have you lost your wits to walk in friendship with this
man who comes full armed upon a friendly mission and
boasts of the power of his country's war bands and doesn't
know the meaning of courtesy?"

He looked at her quickly then and, seeing her unmoving, ordered again, "The ass, Thalamika!"

She didn't, at once, answer him. She walked steadily
to Kretheus and linked her arm in his and stood looking
at Andrios coldly. She watched the remembrance of

laughter leave his eyes, where it had lingered in spite
of Kretheus' threats. She saw his face redden beneath
her stare, saw him begin to scuff the road with his feet
before she said, "Thalamika, daughter of Kalmia of
Phaistos, is no man's lady. Remember? You, yourself,
said it, O Andrios, Lord of Knossos. Don't think *you*
can command me. Come, Kretheus."

They turned, Kretheus grinning at Andrios' discomforting, as the other two men plodded up astride their
weary asses. She didn't turn as Andrios sent her name
after her, pleadingly. Miserably Andrios watched them
go. It would, he knew, have done no good to run after
them, even if he weren't too exhausted. He'd had little
sleep for days, working under pressure to quell a revolt
that threatened in the western provinces. Thalamika
hadn't been far from his thoughts during all those days
and nights. It had been almost as if his thinking about
her had caused her to appear, suddenly, before him on
the road. He'd been so glad to see her and, for a moment,
he'd thought she'd been glad to see him. And then he'd
had to spoil it all.

Why couldn't he remember her pride? Why, for that
matter, couldn't he learn to discipline his own pride, his
own arrogance? The trouble was he never knew when it
would rise in him, but he would, he thought, have been
on guard against it today if he hadn't been so tired and
if Kretheus—Poseidon blast him—hadn't made him so angry. His very love for Thalamika, he thought, made him
impatient with her failure to see that Kretheus was somehow dangerous.

He wished he could stop loving her. He knew her weak-
nesses, her spoiled ways and carelessness of other peo-

ple's wants and needs. But it did no good to dwell upon her faults. There were so many good things about her, and anyway what man in love wanted to analyze his beloved?

He must not stand here. He must get back to Minos with his report. Sometimes he wished he'd been born a poor peasant instead of nephew to the Priest-King. Or that his uncle had left him alone to follow his father's profession instead of snatching him from his pleasant life to train him in statesmanship. He looked at the two men waiting for him upon their patient asses and felt a sudden distaste for their company and handed his own ass to one of them and left the road for a path across a barley field that would bring him to Knossos without the need to travel with his companions.

Thalamika had looked once furtively over her shoulder, but the curve in the road hid Andrios from her. She listened to Kretheus reliving the scene they'd just played, chuckling at the memory of her words and actions, his good humor entirely restored, and wondered why her heart seemed to hurt and her spirit to feel beaten.

Kretheus sensed her mood after a time and set himself to cajole her out of it. Before the red and blue pillars of the House of the Priest-King came in sight, she was laughing again. He left her at her aunt's and held her hand a long time, saying good-bye, thanking her for the day, making of his words a caress. She'd forgotten Andrios and was singing softly to herself as she stopped to unloose her shoes at the house door.

Drupos met her inside. He was standing beside the stone lamp cracking his knuckles, looking as if he could not make up his mind about something. "Where *have* you been, Thalamika?" he asked angrily as she entered. "The others have come home long ago, and my mother's been worried. I was about to call the Guardians of the Peace to search for you."

"My aunt needn't have worried," she said, sounding indifferent about it. "I was with Kretheus. A goatboy delayed us, and then Andrios came . . ."

"Andrios! Is he back? Where is he?" He looked behind her as if he expected Andrios to appear through the closed door.

"How should I know? I left him in the road by the defile."

"You left him? Left *Andrios* in the road! You . . ."

She was tired and wanted no argument, and she started to brush past him but he caught her arm and held her. "What *is* this, Thalamika? Why didn't Andrios come with you?"

She lifted her shoulders. "He and Kretheus quarreled. Andrios ordered me to mount his ass and come home with him, leaving Kretheus alone. No one orders me about, Drupos. Besides, it would have been unmannerly to desert a guest of the Priest-King who had been my partner at the bull capturing. Andrios presumes upon his friendship for you when he tries to tell me what to do and what not to do, and I won't have it. Andrios is nothing to me. He holds some foolish fear of Kretheus, though . . ."

"Kretheus! Kretheus! I'm sick of the sound of his name. He's put a spell upon you, Thalamika—a spell most likely invoked from one of his outlandish gods. If Andrios fears him, it's with good reason, you may be sure. I wonder . . ." He began to pull at his lower lip, and her irritation faded before curiosity to know what had come into his mind. "Did you tell Andrios of Philona's suspicions, Thalamika?" he asked.

"No. You remember we decided there wasn't any need. Besides, what could Philona's father have to do with Kretheus?"

"That's just what I'm wondering, Thalamika. Maybe . . . Where did you leave Andrios?"

"I told you. Where the defile comes down to the road. That goatboy . . ."

"Poseidon take the goatboy! I'm going to find Andrios."

He was out of the door before she could put another question to him. She turned away, not bothering to think any more about him or Andrios. It had been a long day, a difficult day, and she was aware, as she had never been before, of her weary body and went slowly up the stairs and lay upon the soft skins of her bed, not even taking off her dress.

Drupos started at his ordinary walking pace to meet Andrios, trying to piece together the hints of trouble until they would make some kind of picture. Philona's fears. A peaceful embassy coming to Minos in arms. Certain vague whisperings he'd heard and paid no heed to, whisperings about Kretheus. What had they been? The Mycenean had been seen in strange places, dark-cloaked and late at night. Something beyond that, too, some hint of treachery. Why hadn't he paid more attention?

There were other things, too. Andrios' suspicions of Kretheus. Unrest among the farmers. Especially Andrios' suspicions. Andrios was not accustomed to deal in fancies. Yet, could it be that Andrios, hard-driven by his unwanted love for Thalamika, was merely jealous of the tall and handsome visitor, who had so clearly enthralled the girl? By the Labrys, he'd like to shake some sense, some decorum into her. Flinging herself at Kretheus for anybody to see. Meeting him in secret corners like a serving maid. Had she no thought for anything but her own will? She was spoiled, yes, but she was supposed to have one of the most intelligent minds among the young men and women at Court. She was far brighter than he. But even he could see that she was behaving foolishly over this Mycenean.

His mind was tired with thinking. He wished he could forget these problems and spend all his time on the Field of Exercise or in the Court of the Boxers, where there was no need to cudgel his brains about matters beyond his understanding. If it hadn't been for Phelleus and his treatment of Philona, he'd never have been dragged into this mad whirlpool of politics and hints of schemes to bring trouble to Crete. But there was danger to Philona —he was still convinced of it in spite of Andrios and Thalamika—and in some strange way her danger seemed to be linked to the Mycenean embassy and Kretheus. If he could just find Andrios, it would all probably come clear. Andrios was wise and, unlike Thalamika, patient with his stupidity. He looked along the empty road, stretching straight into the west. Where *was* Andrios? He should certainly be in sight but he was not.

Worry rose in his mind and winged his feet until he was running along the road in the easy, ground-eating lope of the trained athlete. He didn't see Andrios plodding across the field.

"Drupos!"

The call from the path stopped Drupos and turned him

about. He looked toward the sound and saw Andrios, his riding cloak thrown over his shoulder; his kilts, usually immaculate, pulled awry and grimed with wet and dirt where he'd stumbled in his weariness as he crossed a little stream.

"Andrios! I was coming to find you. What are you doing here? Thalamika said you were riding on the road."

"Thalamika." Drupos could hardly credit the pain in Andrios' voice and eyes. Andrios, from the time he'd been a bull leaper, had learned not to show emotion. He must have sensed the shock to Drupos, for he smiled quickly and came onto the road and took Drupos' arm in greeting. "Forgive me, Drupos. I'm tired and Thalamika . . ." He left it there and dropped Drupos' arm and went on. "What's the matter? Has something—some evil . . ."

"No," Drupos reassured him, not waiting for the end of the sentence. "All's well in Knossos, or was when I left it a quarter hour ago. Look over there, Andrios. Somebody's left a farm cart in the field. Come sit with me awhile, and I'll explain why I came to meet you."

Andrios said, "Yes. I don't think I can go much further without a rest. I've walked and ridden far this week and talked until my throat aches and slept little. Minos will be waiting, but he'll have to wait a little longer."

He hoisted himself up onto the cart and found it full of hay, fragrant with mint and wild thyme cut with it, and stretched himself gratefully upon it. Drupos sat on the cart's edge and swung his legs and told Andrios of Philona's suspicions of her father, of the rumors about Kretheus' night prowls. "And another thing, Andrios," he added, remembering suddenly talks he'd had in the past with Thalamika about the Woman of Mycenae, "though I don't know whether it's important. Thalamika distrusts the Queen. It's not just dislike, Andrios. Thalamika's likes and dislikes are too wayward to cause anyone worry. But this is different, something deeper and more troubling. Thalamika says the Queen talks always of hatred for Crete and prays her god, Zeus, to send his anger against our land to destroy it. But when Minos comes into her Hall or when she looks down upon him as he administers justice according to the laws or receives embassies in the Audience Chamber, then, as at any time when he might see her face, the Queen shows it only soft and smiling and speaks lovingly of Crete and its people."

Andrios sat up slowly. "Yes," he said. "I, too, mistrust the Queen. Since Minos took the boy from her charge to train him, she's been a little—mad, I think. She was teaching Sarpedon to hate Crete or was trying to, though his love for his father spoiled her plans. And even up to a year ago something, or somebody, was poisoning the boy's thoughts. That was why Minos asked me to take the Young Prince in hand, for Minos has too little time to be with him and thought the lad should be taught by someone of his own house. Even as Minos himself is now teaching me."

"But if Minos knows these things, why doesn't he send the Queen back to her brother?"

"Now, Drupos, think. Minos knows only that the boy was restless and unhappy, laggard in his studies and careless about training his body on the Field of Exercise. The Priest-King knows little about his Queen. He's too besotted with her. He won't hear a word against her, and those who've tried a hint have wished they'd governed their tongues more carefully. Without proof, solid proof, I don't dare charge the Queen with anything. And indeed I can't see even now a clear need to speak. The boy—I'll swear it upon the shrine of The Goddess—no one can harm the boy's mind now. And how could Myrtis bring danger upon the land or Minos, except through Sarpedon? Poseidon! I wish I could see some clear pattern in all these doubts. Look, Drupos. Let's go over them again. One: the Myceneans come in arms upon a peaceful mission. But they've shown no armor since, and it may be all this talk and warlike display was no more than a whim of their leader, who seems to be overzealous for war. Two: the Mycenean merchants come, Philona charges by stealth, to the House of Phelleus. But we've only Philona's word that they were stealthy, and she's angry because her father keeps her prisoner. She may see plots where none exist. Besides, Phelleus *is* chief of the merchants, and they would naturally consult with him about their common concerns. Three: Kretheus." He seemed to choke a little on the name. "Kretheus had to be stopped from dishonoring The Goddess and jeers at what he chooses to call our softness and love of luxury. But who can say he doesn't honor his own gods? And jeers aren't threats. Every man is entitled to his own opinion of the way of life of an alien people. Four: you've heard Kretheus is seen late at night and skulking in a dark cloak in Amnisos. Well, when hasn't it been true that men have sought pleasures in the dark they wouldn't be proud to own by daylight?"

He beat his forehead with the palm of his hand, as

if by violence he would clear his brain. "Cobwebs, Drupos. All cobwebs that fall away to nothing when you try to hold them. And yet, I *am* afraid, for us and for Philona and for Crete, I feel a sure warning of danger as if Poseidon himself were pricking me with his trident." He sighed and shook his head. "Well, the time has come to talk to Minos and tell him of my fears, though I'd give my very sealstone to take him proof of them."

He pushed himself off the cart and Drupos jumped down beside him, and together they started silently toward Knossos. They parted at the south entrance. Drupos told Andrios he'd found a slave of Phelleus, who for a large bribe had promised to arrange for him to talk to Philona at sunset, and he was going down to the port. "When will you tell Minos, Andrios?" he asked as he left.

"Tonight. When I've bathed and changed my clothes and had some food and wine. I'll tell him and it may be he'll explain some of the things that worry us, for he has many spies in his service and countless reports of what's happening in his realm and indeed in the whole world."

CHAPTER
EIGHT

Andrios went slowly to his own quarters in the House of the Priest-King, grateful that this was the hour for the evening meal. He met few people in the Central Court, and those he saw were too hurried to stop him. He paused once on his way to speak to one of the Nubian Guards and send a message to Minos. He wished he could go on to his father's house. He'd like his father's cool judgment upon the things Drupos had told him, but the house of the Chief Fresco Painter was beyond the other end of the Palace. It would take him half an hour just coming and going, and he mustn't keep Minos waiting longer than absolutely necessary.

He dropped his filthy kilts in the middle of his room and spent the better part of an hour soaking his tired muscles in a clay tub decorated with paintings of octopi and flying fish, and filled to the top with steaming water sweetened by oils perfumed with spices brought from the East. He closed his eyes and felt the warmth relax his body, while his bath attendant scraped away the itchy stubble from his face with an obsidian razor. By the time the attendant handed him scarlet kilts, deep bordered in blue, and cinched tight the silver belt that went with them, Andrios had almost forgotten tiredness and was ready for the spitted partridge, dripping with a tangy sauce and brought hot from the kitchen brazier. A bowl of olives, a round loaf of crusty bread, and a cup of wine, well watered, made up the rest of his meal and he ate it with good appetite.

The food further refreshed him and he came to the antechamber of the small Throne Room in the Palace, feeling ready for his talk with the Priest-King. His friend Nitos, Captain of the Nubian Guard, saluted him and said Minos was waiting. Andrios dipped his hands into the great bowl set in the floor, splashed a little fresh water upon his face and head and bare feet in the ritual lustration required of all who entered the Throne Room, and opened the door.

Light flared from oil lamps set in niches about the room, which was empty except for the Priest-King. Andrios was glad none of the royal ministers were here tonight. What he must say to Minos shouldn't be heard by other ears, no matter how loyal.

Minos sat upon a high-backed stone chair, cushioned for comfort, toying with a small ivory figure of a bull leaper in the act of somersaulting over the back of a bull. He didn't, at once, see Andrios, and the younger man watched him affectionately, distressed by the sadness upon the face of the man accounted chief among the lords of all the lands that bordered the Great Green Sea. Truly, Andrios thought, being a king didn't always bring happiness. Was Minos mourning the loss of the princes and princesses the Queen had borne him? Six of his children had been stillborn or had died before they were a year old—all except Sarpedon, who had been the first.

The Young Prince, thank The Goddess, was strong-limbed and, since he was no longer badgered and beat upon by his mother's will, strong-minded too and happy-souled.

Or was the Priest-King brooding upon the willfulness of his people or upon some other problem of his rule he hadn't made plain to Andrios? Andrios sighed, wishing again he'd not been singled out for special training in matters of state. It was an honor, of course, to be so chosen, but his life would have been pleasanter if he could have lived it as the other young men and women in the Palace lived, with time for laughter and time for painting frescoes as his father did.

Minos lifted his head and saw Andrios and smiled. "So, you've come, nephew. I was beginning to fear you'd forgotten me."

The tone of the voice denied his words, and Andrios knew he was being teased. But he answered gravely, as befitted a servant of the Priest-King, and came into the room to a low olivewood stool with tiny carvings of the sacred bull horns, the Horns of Consecration, upon it. Standing beside the stool, he said, "I waited only, O Minos, to wash away the road dust and put on clean clothes before coming to your presence."

"Sit down, sit down, boy, and don't be so solemn," Minos said, and when Andrios was seated added, "Now tell me what you found in the west. Is it as bad as we'd heard?"

Andrios told him that the farmers in the western parts of the island were grumbling at the increased taxes and had made trouble for the tax gatherers. There'd been stonings and burnings, but the trouble seemed to be contained in one small area, and the token guard Andrios had taken with him and left stationed there would, he thought, set all right again. "The trouble, O Minos," he went on, "lies in this. The people in the west have had two bad harvests and are hard-pressed. I think it would be wise if you could order your tax gatherers to forgive these farmers a portion of your due until the next crop."

Minos shifted restlessly upon his throne, his face as heavy as his ponderous body, and Andrios thought what have I said to bring the look of thunder to his face? and waited, knowing better than to speak further until Minos gave him leave. The silence grew between them, and Andrios willed his body, sensible of tiredness once more, to stillness.

At last Minos spoke. "I'll open my mind to you, Andrios, for you must know all that I know and fear and suspect. I must depend on you to protect my son and guide him if—if it be the will of The Goddess that I surrender her my spirit before Sarpedon is a man grown."

"Do not say so, O Minos," Andrios began, but the Priest-King held up his hand and his nephew was silent again.

"Speaking of death won't bring it nearer, Andrios," he said and smiled bleakly, "and it's well to be forearmed. For who can know when death will come? You are of my house, and it's not impossible that you might sit one day upon this throne if Sarpedon too . . . But no more of that! You're an apt pupil in learning to govern men. You have a—a sense of administration not given to many so young as you. And in any case you will one day be chief among the leaders in Crete. It's time then that you know more than I've told you in the past. So hear me, Andrios."

Andrios was depressed by his uncle's words, but he also wanted to bring some comfort to the heavily burdened King. He dropped the more formal address in answering and said, "I'm listening, Brother of my Mother."

"There's trouble in Crete, Andrios. It's not only the trouble over taxes; the hectares of grain and jars of oil, the goats and sheep and asses I must have for the well ordering of my government and the welfare of my people. It's not only a bad harvest here and a plague upon animals there. I judge your report good and I will, as you advise, ease somewhat—as much as I can in safety—the assessments in the west. But this isn't the core of the matter. People always grumble at paying taxes, not knowing it's those levies that, spent in their behalf, keep the land peaceful, their homes safe and the seaways free of pirates who, if they were let, would ruin the very trade that keeps the grumblers prosperous. But this—this spilling over of complaint into violence is something more, plainly the work of some person or faction blowing hard upon a little fire and fanning it into a mighty flame. And all my agents, trusted men, trained to hear and see in secret places and secret ways, cannot find who's doing it."

"Who among us, O Minos, *would* do such a thing?"

"Who indeed, Andrios?" Minos spoke dryly. "If I knew that, my sleep wouldn't be troubled at night and my mind clouded with worry by day."

"May I say out what's in my mind, O Minos?"

"Say on."

Andrios wished he didn't have to speak. He didn't like

rumor bearing and he had, he knew, nothing except rumors. But he didn't think he could wait for proof. Proof might not come until it was too late. He gave the Priest-King the gist of all his talk with Drupos, keeping to himself only those things they had said of Myrtis, the Queen.

Minos listened, his body still, his face shaded by his hand. When Andrios was done the Priest-King dropped his hand and looked a long time at his nephew. The boy must know, he thought, though he wished it weren't necessary. Andrios was too young to be burdened with these state troubles. He should be spending the days of his youth as the others of his age spent theirs; free from care, taking joy in each day's pleasures, singing and dancing through each evening's hours, not going about upon missions for the country and sharing the woes of the Priest-King. But, Minos reminded himself, there was no one else of his house. If his brother had lived . . .

"Kretheus and the embassy from Mycenae," he said aloud. "You distrust them?"

"Yes, though I cannot say just why."

"I don't believe they mean us active harm, Andrios. Not Kretheus and the men with him, though they flaunt their arms and play at soldiers even here, where all is peace and our men don't study war. And I'm not afraid of the merchants of Mycenae, who have lived so long among us and prospered because we have made the seaways safe from the Land of the Pharaohs to the country where, if I'm to believe my sea captains, the sun always shines in summer and there is no night. These merchants who live among us don't, I'm sure, like us much. They are greedy and want to use our harbors and our honest weights without payment of port duties. But they too, like our farmers, are only grumblers and won't do anything as long as their merchant ships bring cargoes from the whole world to be traded again and again in our market places. Even Phelleus, though he hates us as his daughter says, wouldn't, I think, attempt to challenge my authority.

"But Mycenae herself. There's another matter. My father, when he was Priest-King, tried to give me his wisdom. And when he felt his own life coming near its end, he warned me against the Myceneans. They are a strong and warlike people and bitter in their jealousy of all who have more than they have. And their King is ambitious. My father wanted the Myceneans as friends not enemies, and he arranged for me to take their princess as wife and I went to Mycenae and brought home my Myrtis" —his voice softened—"to be Queen of Crete when I should succeed my father as Priest-King."

He paused then and looked over Andrios' head as if he were looking into the past, and again Andrios waited. When Minos began to speak again the softness was gone from his voice. "There was a time of good will between us then. Many of our artisans went to Mycenae to bring beauty and some luxury to the harsh court of the King in his hill fortress, and many of their merchants came here. Then the Old King died and the tomb of his ancestors was opened to receive him, and his son, the brother of my wife, took the throne. King Lyssus is young and vigorous. He doesn't like our swift, well-armed ships that control the Great Green Sea and bring its wealth to us. He's sent this embassy to seek better trading terms for his merchants, and I may make a show of giving him what he seeks. But he's also jealous of our wealth and our artists, though he pretends to scoff at them. He would, if he could, send an army to conquer us and make us subject to him, but he knows that without a war fleet he'd never land his army here, for our sailors would stop him."

Andrios had been listening carefully, not interrupting, but he couldn't keep still any longer. "That, O Minos," he said, "is why I fear the arms-bearing Kretheus and his companions. They are not a peaceful embassy but trained warriors. Suppose the Mycenean merchants in Crete have secretly armed and are ready to attack Knossos and . . ."

"To what end, Andrios? They might, in truth, seize the Palace. They might even hold it for a time. But not for long. My sailors are loyal—loyal to my house and to the land, and especially to the rich pay they wouldn't get anywhere else. Unless King Lyssus can follow up a sudden attack with a fleet of warships, he wouldn't be so foolish as to allow an uprising among his merchants here and so give warning about his thinking."

"And Lyssus has no fleet?"

"Unless he has the power to make his ships invisible, he has none. Our people in Mycenae say there are no ships being built on the shores of the Sea of Argos except for the usual trade ships. And my spies report there are no war argosies fitting out in the islands that own allegiance to Mycenae. No signal fires have been lit upon the headlands to summon freemen from their fields to come in arms to the gathering places. No, Andrios, Lyssus isn't ready. And that, thank The Goddess, gives me time. Time to bring my people to see their danger;

time to teach the young men the ways of war and the old men and women how to survive if war must come; time to build up a store of spears and war swords and shields, body armor and helmets. Already the armorers are working in a secret place, known only to me and the Chief Armorer. Already the store of arms is growing. And, when the month of storms is here again and the sailors are home from the sea, I'll set them to work making soldiers of our boxers and wrestlers, our shepherds and goatboys, even of our bull leapers." His face flushed and he struck his knees with his fists and said, "Poseidon! Why must men fight? Why can't Lyssus be content to govern his own country and set his mind and the minds of his people to peace? But he will not and I—I must go his way and turn my peaceful, happy people into warriors, or this land will surely die."

Andrios felt as if the whole mighty Palace weighed upon him. War! How long had it been since the people of Crete had thought of war? There had been troubles; famine; sickness among men and animals; even earthquakes, some so severe as to destroy the great palaces in whole or in part. But the fields had yielded rich harvests again. The sickness had, in time, passed from the people and the beasts. The palaces had been rebuilt, more stately and beautiful than before. But war was a different kind of trouble. War destroyed more than land and wealth and buildings. It burned into men's very souls and left them seared for at least a generation. He'd heard tales of war from old men whose grandfathers had learned them from a terrified few who had escaped to Crete when the barbarian ancestors of the Myceneans had first appeared in the land across the Great Green Sea.

He hated the thought of war but he hated more the thought of being conquered by the Myceneans, made subject to their king and their fierce gods, and he was afraid. He doubted Minos could whip the people of Crete to war. They had no fear of Mycenae. The sea itself was, they thought, their protector, better than any fortifications made by men; the sea and the war ships that patrolled it. His people, he himself, wanted nothing to do with war. They were, even as Kretheus had charged, soft with generations of good living and the love of ease and beautiful things. They loved gaiety too and luxury and were accustomed to it. Even the small farmers lived better than most of the princes of the Argolis. If the people in the country and the little towns complained of taxes, what would they do if they were ordered to leave their homes and fields and olive groves and flocks of sheep and goats to become soldiers?

"Yes, Andrios," Minos said, seeing, as he often did, into the minds of the people with him, "it will be hard. But it must be done. Given time, it can be done. Be thankful that Lyssus is laggard still. But this—this disaffection at home adds to the problem. We *must* know who is fostering it. My regular spies haven't been able to find out. Maybe you can succeed where they failed."

Andrios thought the King was catching at straws. He doubted he could do anything more than the trained agents who knew more of spying than he would ever do. But there was no use telling his uncle that. He got up from the stool and said, "I'll do what I can, O Minos," and Minos put his hand for a moment on his nephew's arms before he said, "Thank you, Andrios, and good night."

Andrios turned to leave the throne room. At the door he looked back and saw that Minos had taken up the ivory bull leaper. His hand squeezed the delicate figure as if it had been the neck of King Lyssus of Mycenae until the ivory snapped and fell in two pieces to the stone floor. Minos opened his hands and closed them again, but as Andrios went through the door he felt sure the Priest-King had no knowledge of what he had done.

CHAPTER
NINE

The afternoon sun flooded the broad level space below the House of the Priest-King. A little wind from the sea tempered the heat to scores of people leaning upon a stout wooden barrier, breast-high, that surrounded a quadrangle of turf, tramped and torn by bulls' hoofs. A month and a half had passed since Thalamika had stood upon the shore at Amnisos to welcome the embassy from Mycenae. Today she was part of a continuing stream of merchants and farmers, craftsmen and servants, men and women of all ages going to the place set aside for taming the wild bulls who had been kept since their capture in the bull pens beneath the Palace.

She found a spot at one of the short sides of the quadrangle, but, unlike the others, she hadn't come to see the bull leapers pit their skill and will against the anger of the bulls. She'd come to find Kretheus, thinking he would surely be here today.

She hadn't seen him for a week past, though she had, at the end of it, deliberately haunted the places in the sprawling, winding Palace where she thought he might be. For three weeks after the bull capturing she'd seen him every day. She herself was, happily, still in the

Queen's disgrace and banned from the Queen's apartments. She knew there were whisperings and wonderings as gossip flew about the Palace, but she cared little so long as she was free to govern her own time.

She'd spent much of it with Kretheus. As much as she could. She found she couldn't command his company as she'd been accustomed to do with most of the men of the Palace. He wouldn't come at her bidding. He would appear suddenly, as if he'd just dropped a cloak of invisibility, calling for her at her aunt's house or coming up beside her as she talked to Thalia or the small, frightened Amphidora or another of the young girls who lived in the Palace. He would listen to their talk, courteous but withdrawn, until he could separate her from her friends and take her off.

Sometimes they went to the harbor and stood upon the shore while men unloaded merchant ships from distant lands. She loved the long, slim vessels, high-prowed, each with its own special symbol at the tall center mast. He was full of questions and she answered him gladly, proud of her knowledge. What was the full complement of rowers in a war galley? How were they armed? How many vessels were equipped with battering rams? How far north did the Cretan ships trade and how long would such a voyage take? Were the trading ships protected by war vessels? How were the sailors occupied in the season of storms when they couldn't go about their usual business? What cargoes were traded with what lands?

Once or twice he left her to talk to the captain of a vessel which had just been beached, ready for unloading, upon the wide and sandy shore. Once he called her over to hear the tale of a man who'd been gone from

Amnisos four years, sailing always north, hugging the shoreline against danger from sudden storms that often lashed in from the wide western waters, trading cargo for cargo and always for gain. The captain was impatient to see his wife and children in the town, but he answered Kretheus' questions courteously and repeated courteously for Thalamika his tale of a country far to the north. It was, he said, a land of mists and small rains and wide forests, where the people were building a mighty shrine to their god; a shrine of huge stones—many cubits higher than the tallest man—placed in a circle and dedicated to the worship of the Sun. He told them, a suggestion of awe and wonder still in his mind as he talked, how he had found upon the base of some of the stones, incised into the hard rock, their own double-ax symbol. He had, by signs and a few words of the strangers' language, asked the meaning of the sign and learned that these people knew The Goddess and reverenced Her and did Her honor along with their own strange northern gods.

At other times Kretheus had led her up into the hills, where they gathered armfuls of gold and blue flowers or explored one of the myriad caves that stretched deep into the mountain rock. Once they had passed a tree shrine and she'd turned aside into the sacred enclosure and lifted her arms to the Lady of the Trees. But she'd been careful not to pass that way again, for Kretheus had stood by scowling, and been cross for the rest of the afternoon. He said he couldn't understand why the Cretans didn't worship their deity properly, in temples of stone as the Myceneans did, and when she tried to tell him that The Goddess preferred open places or small house shrines watched over by her sacred snakes, he wouldn't listen and walked away from her. Sometimes it seemed to her that anything to do with The Goddess angered him.

She'd felt surer and surer, on these expeditions, that he wanted her for his lady and she'd waited to hear him ask her to return with him to Mycenae and keep his hearth forever. But, though he sometimes paid her compliments and sometimes teased her as she'd heard Drupos tease Philona; though his voice and words sometimes hinted at love, he hadn't spoken of taking her back with him to Mycenae.

And now, for a week, he'd deserted her, avoiding even speaking to her when their ways might have crossed in the House of the Priest-King. Or so it seemed to her. Hope had struggled to survive that week of loneliness, of wondering where he was and aching even for a sight of him. She'd fed her heart with assurances that he was only caught up in the business that had brought him to Knossos, and comforted hope with memories of his love hints. But today assurances and comfort had failed, and she'd banished her pride and come to seek him where she felt sure he would be.

She looked again around the rectangle. She thought all Knossos must be here, leaning against the barricade. Maybe he'd come while she was busy remembering and she hadn't seen him. Drupos was there, and Andrios frowning at something as usual. She'd avoided Andrios since their meeting upon the road as, she thought, he'd avoided her. She looked away quickly now, having no wish to meet his eyes. Thalia was there, laughing with Spyros. They saw Thalamika and waved and beckoned, but she pretended not to see.

Kretheus was not leaning anywhere on the barricade. "The Goddess bless you, O Lady Thalamika."

Thalamika jumped and looked toward the sound of the words, and saw the Young Prince Sarpedon standing tiptoe beside her.

"All glory to The Goddess," she answered automatically. "You startled me, Sarpedon. I didn't hear you come."

"I'm sorry, Lady Thalamika. I didn't mean to make you jump. Is the bull taming going well?"

He was so full of eager happiness she smiled in spite of the sadness in her mind. "To tell the truth, Sarpedon," she said, "I haven't been watching."

"Not watching the bull taming!" He couldn't have sounded more unbelieving if she'd said she'd stopped breathing.

"No." She grinned at him. "I came to find Kretheus."

He made a face as if the name were distasteful to him and said, "Why, O Lady Thalamika? Why do you come looking for someone who would have profaned The Goddess if Andrios and I hadn't forced him to be quiet?" His brown eyes had lost their sparkle and become grave, and he watched her face seriously.

She felt a fresh rush of anger for Andrios because he'd tried to turn the Young Prince's mind against the Mycenean. She thought she must set the boy straight again and she said, gently, "Profane The Goddess? I'm sure you're wrong, Sarpedon. No man would offer sacrilege knowingly to a divinity, even if he didn't worship her. Remember, Sarpedon, Kretheus is a Mycenean recently come to our land and doesn't know our ways. It's a pity," she added and, in spite of her affection for the

Young Prince, her voice was waspish, "that Andrios had to force our guest when a warning spoken in his ear would have done as well."

"No, Lady Thalamika!" Sarpedon almost tripped on his own words in his wish to justify Andrios. "You have it wrong. I was close to Andrios and I heard him give just such a warning, and in the Mycenean tongue too, when Kretheus first lifted his hand to the olive crown. Kretheus looked at him with a look so—so *evil* you couldn't believe it and took the olive crown from his head. It was then—not before—Andrios pinioned him and, seeing Kretheus about to speak, bade me cover his mouth with my hand."

She was, for a flick of time, stunned by what she'd heard. Then her mind turned about and she said, "We mustn't forget, Sarpedon, that Andrios isn't a Mycenean and, though he knows their language a little, he isn't easy in it. Surely Kretheus just didn't understand the warning."

Sarpedon was shaking his head violently. Though he wouldn't interrupt a lady with words, he had to show his disagreement somehow. As soon as she stopped speaking he said, "No, Lady Thalamika. You've got it all wrong. It wasn't like that at all. Kretheus *did* understand."

"But, Sarpedon," she argued carefully, "no one would . . ."

"Please, Lady Thalamika, *please* listen. Andrios, too, was afraid his Mycenean words hadn't been plain to Kretheus. He doesn't like Kretheus, but Andrios would never offer an insult to a guest of my father. He waited for Kretheus when the dancing was over. I was with him and heard him apologize, explaining so slowly and carefully even I understood each word, that we thought it an act of sacrilege to salute a Priestess who danced in honor of The Goddess. And then, Lady Thalamika, then Kretheus laughed an ugly-sounding laugh with no gaiety in it and answered in our own Cretan language and said he was no dullard. He said it was so in all lands. And then he said the Myceneans had no reason to revere our Goddess. He said they worshiped *gods,* like Zeus and Poseidon in proper temples. He said he feared no goddess of a foreign people, least of all our Lady and owed Her no reverence. He said—he said," the young voice stumbled at the recollection of what he was about to repeat, "that if any woman were worthy of a man's reverence, it would be such a one as you. So, you see, O Lady Thalamika, Andrios was *not* at fault."

The Young Prince's words seemed to beat at Thalamika. She wouldn't believe what she heard. Yet her horror at the very thought of such deliberate defiance offered a deity—any deity—warned her she did believe. The boy beside her seemed to sense her thought, for he spoke again quietly. "I didn't dream these things, O Lady Thalamika. Andrios will bear me out."

She looked at him without seeing him, shaken by shame for Kretheus and dread that The Goddess would punish them all for his words; by anger at Andrios that he'd turned from her when she'd spoken to him after the dancing, turned away in hurt pride instead of telling her these things then, when he might have saved her from this creeping love for the Mycenean; more than all else by the knowledge that her heart wouldn't be swayed from its yearning for Kretheus by what she'd just heard and must believe. What must she do? What *could* she do?

Sarpedon laid his hand upon her arm. "I'm sorry, Lady Thalamika," he said with dignity that would have become a man three times his age, "I didn't mean to bring sorrow to you. But it's right you should know the truth about the Mycenean and not blame Andrios falsely."

She patted his hand absently, not really hearing his words but hearing the sound of apology, and turned from him and moved, unseeing, away from the barricade. He watched her go, troubled by her distress, then forgot her when a bull, released from its tether, thundered through a gate in the barrier toward a bull leaper waiting to grapple and tame him.

Thalamika didn't hear the bull's bellow nor the sound of its beating hoofs. She didn't know as yet what she was doing or where she was going. Her feet took her, unbidden by her mind, along the path that wandered among grass and flowers up the slope to the House of the Priest-King. "Kretheus, Kretheus, Kretheus," her mind said and her despairing heart answered, "Oh, Kretheus."

She reached the very edge of the West Court before she knew she had to find him. She pushed her way among the sellers of olive oil and grain, sheep and young kids, sealstones and pottery, and went to the Hall of the Strangers, where the embassy was lodged. It was empty, not even a slave guarding the doors that stood wide open to catch the breeze. She called his name and got no answer, and sought him in the Hall of the Men and in the courts and corridors and workshops, but she couldn't find him. She went to the Grand Staircase, thinking he might be in one of the lesser courts on the lower floor. Water from last night's rain still overflowed the basins set among the drains so cunningly made to control the storms, and the sound of its rushing seemed to drum the name of Kretheus.

Then, as if The Goddess had brought him out of sound into sight, Thalamika saw him: saw him where he had no reason to be, hurrying, huddled into a dark mantle, looking often over his shoulder, down the corridor that led to the Queen's Hall.

Thalamika slid into an angle in the corridor wall made for holding a standing lamp which had been removed for cleaning. There she could see him yet remain herself unseen, and she watched him as he took a final swift look behind and went into the quarters of the Woman of Mycenae. Thalamika almost forgot her anguish in curiosity. What was he about? There was no rule to say that men couldn't visit the Queen's Hall. But in fact they seldom did, except Minos who came and went as he would. Few men of Knossos had been in these apartments nor had any reason to be. Certainly no foreign ambassador should have cause to come to the Queen by stealth.

Thalamika moved quickly. Her bare feet made no sound on the smooth stones of the stairway leading into a little, enclosed room that looked down into the Queen's Hall. Thalamika flattened her body against the side of the opening. She wouldn't, she thought, be noticed by anyone below, for she'd worn a dark dress today and it blended into the shadows.

She could see the length of the room beneath her and she was puzzled, for it seemed to be empty. She moved forward cautiously and heard a murmur of voices and guessed the Queen and Kretheus were whispering, alone, hidden by the overhang of her hiding place.

At first she could make out no words, for her ears were still tuned to normal sounds. She held her breath, straining to shut away the little noises that fill a quiet room, until she could understand some of what the two were saying. Thank The Goddess her father had insisted she learn the Mycenean language!

The Queen asked, "But when, Kretheus, when would you have me . . . ?"

Kretheus interrupted impatiently. "I can't say, Cousin Myrtis. Not now. Not yet. I'll come myself or send word when all's ready. It won't be long. The hour will depend . . ."

It was the Queen who interrupted this time. "What of the girl, Thalamika? You spend too much time with her. She will likely ruin everything."

He laughed. "Forget the girl, Myrtis. I know what I'm doing there. The little fool—stupid, forward wench she is too—is besotted. She'll do as I say. Her mind's already bemused with loving me. I have only to smile at her, or frown, to wind her will about my smallest finger as you wind the wool on your distaff. Besides she's useful. She's already given me much information about Minos' ships. And she'll give me more if I need it."

Thalamika didn't wait to hear anything else. She kept her wits long enough to leave the listening place as quietly as she'd entered it. But once away from it she began to run. She'd never been so furious in her life. Who did he think he was to play with the Lady Thalamika of Phaistos? So he would use her, would he? Make a fool of her? Taking her to the shore and asking her questions! Her mind didn't stop to wonder how he planned to use her answers. She was beyond reasoning, beyond thinking of anything except a way to strike back at him. How could she ever have thought she loved him? She hated him. She dashed at tears of humiliation she felt on her face. She'd make him suffer for treating her so. Somehow she'd make him pay for his treatment. "I'll go to Minos," she said, and didn't know she'd spoken aloud or that she wasn't alone in the long, dim corridor until she felt an arm about her shoulders, stopping her blind running and heard a voice saying quietly, "Why will you go to Minos and what will you tell him, Thalamika?"

"Oh, Andrios," she said, "I hate him, hate, hate him."

"*Hate* him, Thalamika? Hate the Priest-King?"

"Kretheus," she said, and couldn't say anything else for the sobs that were shaking and choking her.

Andrios had realized she was disturbed, but in the afternoon shadows he hadn't seen how much. He looked at her closely now, as she stood shaking against his shoulder, and saw her hair, always so neat, disheveled; her face streaked with tiny runnels of eye blacking mixed with tears. He'd never seen her so distressed and he ached to comfort her, but he didn't dare. She hates Kretheus, he thought. *Kretheus.* His heart was singing with a fierce joy beneath his pity for her.

Someone was moving at the end of the corridor. He'd better get her away. He pushed her limp body gently from him and said, "Someone's coming, Thalamika. I'll take you to a place where we can talk alone. Here, give me your shoes."

CHAPTER
TEN

Andrios' words penetrated the haze of Thalamika's thoughts and set them whirling. She didn't want to see anyone else. It was more than enough that Andrios had found her, though, since he was here, she was grateful for his steadying arm.

"Quickly," she said and started forward, and he said, "Not that way," and led her through a door so cunningly set in the corridor wall she'd never guessed it was there. He shut the door softly. She only knew it was closed by the difference in the feel of the air. "Wait," he whispered, and she stood still in blackness. She felt something soft and damp against her face and almost cried out, but Andrios came back with a lighted lamp and she saw the soft, damp thing was only a bit of cobweb.

They were standing in a sort of anteroom, empty except for the lairs of myriads of spiders. Andrios, still whispering, explained, "Entrance to the hidden storehouses of the labyrinth. Come." She followed him across the small room and through another door and along a space so shadowed she couldn't tell what it was. He walked quickly ahead of her, holding the lamp behind him to light her way, his own steps sure on the packed earth. She had to run to keep up with him, and the extra effort warmed her body that had been cold with the shock of what she'd overheard. After a time they came into another, larger room. A score of lamps burned in niches in the rock wall and were reflected back in a million points of colored lights from jewels in the open mouths of giant pithoi set around the sides of the room. She reached out and touched one of the mammoth clay jars and found it cool and wet.

"Where—where *are* we, Andrios?" she whispered, and he was glad that she was showing normal curiosity. He answered in his ordinary voice that seemed overloud in this secret place. "Deep beneath the Throne Room, Thalamika. This is the secret treasury of the Priest-Kings, and is known to only a few of us in the Palace. You shouldn't be here, but I couldn't think of any other way to get you out of the corridor quickly. We'll not stay and you must forget you saw it and forget the way to it."

"I couldn't ever find it again, Andrios," she said, thinking of the winding puzzle of the way they'd come. "It's like a maze."

She was shaking again, and her simple anger at Kretheus was complicated now with a growing sense of shame that she had thrown herself at him and so made it possible for him to humiliate her. "What a fool I've been," she said aloud. Andrios looked at her without sympathy. Yes, he thought grimly, you've surely been a fool. But you wouldn't listen to your friends. Poseidon alone knew just what had happened to her, but whatever it was must have been shocking to cause Thalamika to admit herself a fool. He wondered briefly if he could have saved her unhappiness if he'd told her of Kretheus' behavior after the dancing. Would she have listened and believed him then? He doubted it. He guessed it would have taken more than words from him to shake her out of her sudden infatuation for the Mycenean. No matter. He'd better stop thinking about it and get her somewhere they could talk, so he could find out the whole trouble. He wasn't too sure of the state of his own mind. It had been in turmoil, churning between shamefaced delight that she'd found out the truth about Kretheus and pity for her broken pride.

He took her hand and brought her arm through his and led her along what seemed to her endless miles of corridors that twisted and turned and went off at angles between ranks of pithoi of all sizes, smelling of oil and stored grain and wine and spices and other things she couldn't name. They came, eventually, to a door—an ordinary open door in the wall that bounded the West Court and went through it into the dying day and crossed a grassy patch to a grove of cypress trees where there was a stone bench.

Before them, as they sat down, the House of the Priest-King stretched its mighty length. The sun was poised, an exact glowing ball, at the edge of the world. Its far-reaching fingers of gold touched the Palace gently, like a friend, until the piles of white stone, the red and blue columns, even the starkly forbidding Horns of Consecration above the South Porch glowed and seemed to pulsate with light. She covered her eyes with one arm, unable to bear so much beauty.

The small, childlike gesture went to Andrios' heart. He took the arm away gently, before he said, "Now, Thalamika, tell me what's the matter."

She told him haltingly how Kretheus had tricked her for some hidden purpose of his own to love him, and of how she'd heard him telling the Queen. "He was boasting to—to *that woman* that he could wind my will about his finger. He said he found me useful—*useful*—in answering questions about the kingdom of Minos. As if I were nothing more than a guide. *Oh,* the beast. The self-loving, cruel *beast*. He'll pay for this, Andrios. I'll make him pay for it. I'll go at once to Minos and tell him what I heard—tell him how the Mycenean comes secretly to his Queen. No man can serve Thalamika so and not regret it. I'll go to Minos. *Now!*"

She started up from the bench but Andrios drew her back. "Wait, Thalamika," he said, but she shook his hand from her arm as if she hadn't understood him.

"I'm going, Andrios. Would you want me to leave Kretheus unpunished?"

"Thalamika," he said carefully, remembering not to order her. "Thalamika, first listen to me. Then if you still want to go to Minos, I'll not hinder you. Kretheus will be here tomorrow and many tomorrows. There's plenty of time for you to hear first what I've got to say. No, I don't blame you for wanting him punished, though I must say you've not made his pretense of wooing difficult."

"Don't chide me now, Andrios." Thalamika started to speak with her usual irritation when anyone blamed her, but this time she heard the sound of her words and thought she didn't much like it. "It's easy to be wise when everything's known," she went on, more reasonably. "Say what's in your mind but please don't scold me."

"Tell me first, Thalamika. Are you willing now to believe I've some reason for my doubt of Kretheus?"

"Yes. Sarpedon told me how he behaved after the dancing. I wish . . ." She didn't go on, knowing it futile to wish against the past; thinking in an unaccustomed effort to be really honest with herself that it wouldn't, likely, have made any difference if Andrios had explained more on that day that seemed eons away. He waited for her to finish and when she didn't took up his own talk.

"Then maybe you'll also believe I've feared all along that his—pursuit of you—was part of some plot against the Priest-King and against Crete."

Old habit almost made her lash out at him again, but she caught herself and said quietly, "How could it be? If he's come here meaning harm to us, he must have made his plans before he left Mycenae and he didn't even know I existed until"—her face flushed at the memory of her actions on that day—"until he beached his ships at Amnisos."

"I know, Thalamika. But he's crafty and I'm sure once he was here and saw you so eager for his company he must have changed his plan. Tell me again what he and the Queen said—before they spoke of you."

Thalamika flushed with shame as she repeated the few sentences. Word for word. She wondered if that exact and searing memory would ever be gone from her mind.

Andrios moved restlessly upon the bench and was still again. Birds sang their bedtime songs. A badger stuck his striped face out of his hole and saw them and withdrew to safety below ground. A faint streak of rosy sky marked the place where the sun had been. The Palace darkened in the growing twilight.

"Thalamika." Andrios broke the peaceful evening spell. "If you go to Minos now, you'll gain nothing. He will at best laugh at you, saying you've no one but yourself to blame for what has happened. It's no crime to tease a woman with hints, as Kretheus teased you. Especially if the lady asks for it."

She cried out sharply, though she felt in her heart he was right. In truth her anger at Kretheus had begun to lessen a little as she realized more and more, under Andrios' prodding, how much of what had happened had been her own fault. She thought she was beginning to see herself as other people saw her. But that didn't mean she was ready to give up her plans for vengeance. Although she was a little chastened, she was still Thalamika and she still wanted her own way. "What then?" she asked sullenly. "What can I do?"

"This," he said. "Don't let Kretheus know you've changed toward him. Pretend you're still clay for him to work as he chooses. Watch him. Watch what he does. Listen, in secret if you can, to what he says. If he asks questions, answer him but give him false information. And pretend you've changed your heart about the Queen. Humble yourself before her, fawn upon her if you must, but be sure she recalls you to her service. And watch *her*. In that way you may find something solid to take to Minos, something that will at once bring down his wrath upon Kretheus and serve your vengeance *and* save Crete."

She looked at him with horror. "Andrios!" she said when he stopped speaking. "Andrios, I cannot; I *will* not do these things. How can you ask me after the way they've talked about me?"

He wanted to shake her. He almost forgot his love for her. Wouldn't she ever grow up and stop thinking about herself? Couldn't she even now forget herself and think of Crete? Did she want . . . He stopped his angry thoughts, remembering he hadn't fully and properly explained all that was in his mind. He wondered if he'd ever learn to think before he gave way to anger.

"Listen, Thalamika," he begged. "You must do these things for the sake of the Priest-King and this land we both love. You don't know the danger we all may be in. King Lyssus of Mycenae is growing restless because we control all the trade in the Great Green Sea. He wants that control for himself. And he doesn't like it that his ships must pay heavy tolls to land their cargoes in Crete. Yet, where else can he send his trading fleet if he wants to find in one place goods from all over the world? He doesn't like our power or our wealth or our ability to make beautiful things of gold and ivory and clay and colors. He doesn't like our peace-loving people and thinks us soft. He sits upon his hilltop in Argolis and plans to make us a vassal state."

He paused to take a breath, and she asked, "If Minos knows all this, why doesn't he do something about it?"

"He thinks we have time. His spies tell him Lyssus has no war fleet and, without a war fleet, Minos doesn't think the Myceneans would attempt to subdue us. I'm not sure he's right. I'm not sure there isn't somewhere, somehow, in spite of his spies, a fleet waiting to raid us. There are so many places to hide ships in the islands of the Sea. And I'm not sure Kretheus hasn't come with a plot to seize the Priest-King and Knossos while the foreign merchants secure the port of Amnisos. Kretheus' companions look—have always looked—like a war band to me. Certainly it shouldn't take thirty men to make a trade treaty. And they came in arms. All this may be no more than shadow doubts and shadow fears without substance of truth. I don't know. But we must find out."

"Have you told Minos?"

"Yes. But he's stubborn. He trusts his spies and his own judgment and thinks me overyoung and lacking experience. He hasn't said so, but I can tell from the way he looks at me. If I expect him to believe me, I've got to have proof. Philona's watching her father . . ."

"Philona!" Thalamika said. "But Philona can't do anything. She's not even sent word to the market place these past three weeks."

"Because she knows of your—infatuation—for the Mycenean and she's been none too sure of your loyalty to Crete."

Thalamika put her head in her hands, overcome by awareness of what her conduct had led to. Even Philona didn't trust her. "How do you know Philona's watching Phelleus then?" she asked in a muffled voice.

"Drupos sees her, by some arrangement he has made with one of the house slaves, three times a week."

"How can he?" She didn't want to believe what Andrios had told her about Philona.

"He bribed one of the women who values her hope of buying her freedom more than her life if she must remain a slave," he explained patiently. "He waits at a certain place and, when it's safe, the slave brings him to Philona's window and stands guard while they talk together. Philona's more and more sure something's wrong, but she can't say what. I've even tried to make friends with Kretheus, though I loathe him. But he's wary. He knows I don't like him and he doesn't trust me. Sometimes boys let fall something they've heard at home, and Sarpedon is friendly with the sons of many Mycenean merchants. But, until now, he's brought me nothing useful. So, Thalamika, we've no proof to take to the Priest-King. If we get it at all—and I'm not sure we can—I think it must be through you. From Kretheus or the Queen. Already you've given me one fact I didn't know, that Kretheus and Myrtis are cousins."

He waited, looking at her, hoping he'd roused in her fear for the land and life she loved; hoping she'd somehow, right now, put off her childish waywardness and act with responsibility; hoping but not really believing she would do so.

It was too dark now for him to see her face, and for an aching time he waited, having the good sense to let her alone in her thinking. Lights spotted the House of the Priest-King as lamps were lit one after one in all its halls and chambers and courts. He was hungry and more than a little tired. It had been an exhausting day. Watching the bull taming always made him tense, knowing as he did that before the day was over one of his friends of the Bull Leapers Court might be taken from the field dead or badly hurt. And on top of it had come this hour with Thalamika. He wished she would say something, but she didn't and he waited on.

Thalamika sat unmoving. Her pride and self-confidence had received shock after shock since she'd talked to Sarpedon at the bull taming. She was getting a whole new picture of herself, realizing she'd been, for most of her life, blind and selfish, especially so during the weeks since Kretheus had come to Knossos. She'd gone rushing along her own way, admired, spoiled, flying in anger at anyone who suggested a criticism. She'd treated her friends shamefully and yet they'd been patient and understanding. And now—now Andrios was giving her a chance to make some amends and she'd refused him.

Well, she thought, trying to justify herself to her own mind, she'd *had* to refuse him. How could she pretend nothing had changed between herself and Kretheus? How could she hide her hatred of the Woman of Mycenae? She was no actress. Even if she could bear to try to do what Andrios wanted, she'd never succeed at it.

But she must. She must redeem herself, not only in his eyes but in her own. She must prove to herself she could be a decent person. But how *could* she? She'd lived too long without the disciplines that come from outside or might have come from her own mind and heart. If she were going to accomplish anything now, she'd need help.

"Help me," she prayed in her heart, "Great Mother, Mistress of Earth and Air and Sea, of Beasts and Birds and Flowers, Lady of the Labyrinth, help me. Lend me a little of your wisdom and strength."

There was above her head a little sound, and looking up she saw a dove had settled in one of the cypresses. Even as she looked, the small white bird lifted its wings and was gone and Andrios stirred beside her and turned his face from the House of the Priest-King and said softly, as if he'd been inside her mind, "Don't be afraid to try, Thalamika. Remember, neither Kretheus

nor the Queen knows you heard their talk. People see
in others what they expect to see, and Kretheus would
never think he could lose you. You even heard him say
as much. Myrtis is vain. If you ask her forgiveness, say
you were demon-touched for a while, she'll believe you,
for she cannot think ill of herself."

Thalamika had forgotten Kretheus, forgotten her own
self-searching doubts and fears. She'd called upon The
Goddess and The Goddess had come. She, Herself, in
the form of Her sacred dove had come. And surely it
had been The Goddess who had put into the mind of
Andrios the very words to free Thalamika to action. She
knew what Andrios said was true. She had too often
laughed inside herself because she'd seen how easily
people believed what they wanted to believe. Hadn't she
done so herself to her sorrow? Kretheus wouldn't guess
she'd changed. And the Queen, the foolish, heart-proud
Queen, would believe and accept apologies as she believed
and accepted flattery from her handmaidens, blindly.

Thalamika sat straight upon the bench and pulled at
the skirt of her dress. She could feel a long rent in one
flounce. She'd probably snagged it as they came through
the maze of the storerooms. She put up a hand and found
her hair loose from its pins and straggling. She must
look worse than any servant maid and she was suddenly
hungry. But she was no longer harried by anger. She
knew what she must do—for Crete and the Priest-King,
for Drupos and Andrios and Philona and for herself.
The Goddess was with her and she knew she could do
what Andrios wished.

She found her kerchief and gave it to him. "Wet it for

me at the cistern," she said, and added in her new-found humility, "If you please, Andrios."

His heart jumped at the new kindness in her voice. He took the kerchief, but before he did her bidding he asked soberly, for he was still not sure of her, "Will you— you will help, Thalamika?"

"Yes, Andrios, I'll help," she said, "and—and thank you for—for your patience with me."

CHAPTER
ELEVEN

Thalamika found it was easier to plan to spy upon Kretheus than do it. She haunted all the places in the House of the Priest-King where she used to meet him secretly, but he was never in them. Yet she didn't think he was deliberately avoiding her. She did see him, now and again, strolling about the gardens in the company of his friends from Mycenae or in the Audience Chamber or the Central Court. On these occasions he came to stand near her and whisper words that he made sound as if they held a promise of love. She had all she could do not to pull away from him when he touched her hand or shoulder in a half-caress. But she managed to go on pretending, and in time she could do it without thinking, playing at it as she would play a game with a child. Sometimes she thought it wouldn't have made much difference if she'd slapped his face. He was so sure of his own fascination and charm, so secure in his belief that he had her completely captivated, he would put anything she did down to a momentary fit of pique.

But he didn't seek her out or make any explanation except once, when he said he was for a while caught up in the business that had brought him to Crete and must delay his pleasure in their private meetings. And, after each of the brief, public meetings, he'd simply disappeared. No matter how much she tried, she couldn't find out where he went or what he did. He seemed to have a special talent for losing himself when he didn't want to be found.

She had better fortune with the Queen. She asked for and got an audience with the Woman of Mycenae and, though she almost choked upon the dissembling words, begged forgiveness for past faults and promised in the future to be a better handmaiden to the beautiful and gracious wife of Minos. The Queen, as Andrios had predicted, was flattered and preened herself and, after scolding Thalamika again, gave her grudging permission to return to the Queen's Hall.

But no good came of it. At times all the waiting women, even the two who had come from Mycenae, were sent away from the apartments without explanation or excuse. Each time Thalamika tried to hide in the balconied room, and each time her plans were ruined because she couldn't get free from the Mycenean women, who always seemed to be beside her as she left the Hall. She didn't think they were suspicious of her on the Queen's behalf, but she couldn't be sure and she walked carefully not to give herself away. Once, sneaking back as soon as she could to spy, she's seen a cloaked and hooded figure disappearing around a jog in one of the corridors that led to the kitchens. She was sure it was Kretheus, but by the time she came to the turning the hall was empty and silent.

She knew Drupos and Andrios were having no better success. The three of them met several times beneath the cypresses where they could talk without being overheard, but they were no further ahead than they'd been the day she and Andrios had first talked there. And as the days grew longer and nearer to the time of the first harvest, each of the conspirators felt a greater sense of danger, a greater frustration because they still could not guess at the source of the threat. But she'd seen neither Drupos nor Andrios for the past two or three days.

Andrios, she knew, had been on another of his trips for the Priest-King, checking guard stations along the road to Phaistos. Drupos hadn't been to the Court of the Boxers or slept at home. There was, she thought, as Chryses made her ready this early morning, nothing unusual in any of this. Drupos went his own way and no one questioned him or had since, when he was twelve, he'd changed his boy's smock for a man's kilts and attended the Bull Games for the first time. But she wished she could have talked to him or to Andrios.

She wondered at herself as she went toward the Guest House, where she was going to meet Thalia. The discovery of Kretheus' treachery seemed to have turned her mind right about. In these past ten days she'd come to depend upon Andrios' judgment and intelligence; to look forward to seeing him. When he wasn't overtroubled, he was as fun-loving and happy as any other young Cretan. At times he was still almost pompous, but she was beginning to realize his pompousness was a kind of shield for a gentle heart.

As she came near the humped bridge, a small boy in a blue smock rose up out of the long grass, pushed a dried palm leaf at her, and disappeared again into his hiding place. Thalamika read the words written on the leaf and felt her depression lift a little.

"Come to the meeting place tonight at sundown. Don't fail me. Drupos."

She wondered for a moment why he hadn't come himself to tell her. Or why he didn't wait and tell her at the harvesting. Surely he planned to be there. Nobody would miss the fun and feasting of the first harvest of the year if he could help it. Well, there was never any telling about Drupos. He'd probably explain tonight.

She crumpled the note to powder and dropped the bit of dust over the bridge into the ravine below and looked ahead and saw Thalia motioning her to hurry. She ran lightly to meet a dozen young women beside the Spring Chamber of the Guest Pavilion.

A quarter of an hour later they came to a field of ripe barley beside the road. The yellow grain heads danced before the little wind that swept them again and again in the fresh young day. The sun was not yet high enough to bring discomforting heat but, Thalamika thought, before the day was done they'd be glad for the heap of green palm leaves stacked near the road to be used for sun shades.

People dressed in many colors, men and women and children, had already gathered at the meeting place at the edge of the field or were hurrying along the road and the dozens of paths that led to it. The men carried sickles over their shoulders and were laughing and talking cheerfully as they came up to the Landlord of the Field, who awaited them beneath an ancient elm tree. He was an old man, dressed in ceremonial clothes. A staff with a hooked end leaned against the tree waiting for his use when the procession of the harvesters should begin.

The Landlord greeted each man as he came up and

told them off in pairs to form a line behind three musicians who would sing them to the field. The last pair
of harvesters took their place, the last laggard woman sat,
breathless, at the edge of the field. The road and all the
paths stretched empty beneath the sun.

The Landlord took his staff in his two hands and
raised it three times toward the field, giving thanks to
The Goddess for the fullness of the crop and the rich-
ness of the grain heads. A woman handed him a clay
cup of wine and he poured the libation upon the ground
beside a deep-red lily that grew from the roots of the
elm, and promised to dedicate upon the morrow the first
fruits of this harvest to the Lady of the Labyrinth.

The woman took the empty cup. The Landlord threw
his staff over his right shoulder, and immediately every
harvester did the same with his sickle. The old man took
his place at the head of the procession. One of the musicians lifted a sistrum and set its silver rods jingling rhyth-
mically in their frame. With the first tinkle of sound he
and the two men with him raised the Harvesters' Song.
The Landlord stepped out quickly, and the procession of
men, following the song's beat, began to circle the field.

As the song rose into the sky and laughing face
after laughing face passed before Thalamika, she knew
that, for a time at least, her dark, uncertain thoughts were
lost in this harmony of men and work and the gifts of the
earth; of sun and breeze and happy people assured once
more through the protection of The Goddess, of bread and
oil, clothes and land and seed and the thousands of other
good things a full crop would bring. She felt a surge of
excitement as she thought this same scene was being
played out in field after field all over their island. She

turned to Thalia and, as the last of the harvesters circled the end of the field, took her friend's hand and started a quick-moving dance that all the other young women joined while the older ones sang and clapped out the rhythm.

Thalamika hurried, as the sun was westering, toward the cypress grove. A thread of worry threatened her sense of well-being. Drupos hadn't been at the harvesting. Once she thought she'd recognized the back of his head, but it had been only an artisan in a leather smock. What could have kept him away? He'd been, as they all had, looking forward to gathering the first fruits of the year ever since the long cold time of winter storms began. He wouldn't have missed it if he'd been able to come. Would he be in the grove?

The dying afternoon was very quiet. None of the sound of bustle from the House of the Priest-King reached so far. There were no flutterings or twitterings of birds making ready for the night. Even the small winds had hushed themselves. A field of yellow daisies spread outward from the wall of the West Court. They caught the last of the sun and gave it back in a shower of gold. A small blue bird rose straight up singing as Thalamika came around the edge of the cypresses and stopped, puzzled.

It was dark beneath the trees, but she could see Andrios leaning against the bole of one of them, his blue riding cloak making a lighter patch about his shoulders. He was facing her, his figure outlined in a shaft from the sun. He was talking quietly to someone deeper in the shadows. She supposed it was Drupos, and she started to call out when the light changed and penetrated further into the shadows and showed that the second man wore smock and apron. The edge of a bronze knife flashed as he tossed it from hand to hand.

Her heart began to thump. Who was this strange artisan? What was he doing with Andrios and where was Drupos? She started to go toward them and as she moved Andrios' voice rose sharply upon the end of a sentence ". . . have my life for it," he said and, as he spoke, the light-outlined blade in the artisan's hand flashed upward.

Thalamika thought, he's going to kill Andrios and ran toward the stranger, reaching for the hand that held the knife. Andrios shouted, "Thalamika!" and the artisan turned his head and dropped the knife and stepped aside so that she hurtled past him and against Andrios, who caught and steadied her and turned her, winded and half-dazed, toward the artisan.

"What's the matter with you, Thalamika?" the artisan said, and she stared, her mouth foolishly open, for half a minute before she could find wit to speak. "You," she said then, "*Drupos!* What are you doing in a potter's apron? You *were* at the harvest. I thought—just now I thought you were about to kill Andrios. What . . . ?" She stopped, struggling to bring some order to her confused mind, and Andrios said, "Come over to the bench and we'll explain."

When she was seated with Andrios beside her and Drupos, in his ridiculous clothes and a face that didn't belong to him, squatting in front of the bench, Andrios said, "Tell her, Drupos, just what you told me. I'd like to hear you go over it all again in any case."

Drupos drove the knife into the ground and jerked

it out, again and again while he talked. "As you might have guessed, Thalamika," he began, "the potter's apron is a disguise."

"Why?" she said, but he hushed her with a gesture and went on. "Listen, cousin, and don't interrupt. I should be back in Amnisos now but," he grinned, "the waiting is worth it, because I've learned the disguise is good enough to fool even you."

She nodded, hardly believing even yet that the face with age lines drawn upon it in black, eyes narrowed with dark paint, and mouth widened and thickened with saffron was the face of her cousin.

"For a week," Drupos was saying, "I've been wandering about the Palace and the towns of Knossos and Amnisos, trying to smell out the trouble we all three sense upon every wind. There is, as nearly as I can tell, no—no *feeling* of unease in the Palace or in Knossos. The port is different. Something is—not *right*, not as usual in Amnisos. Again and again before today, I came on little groups of men, merchants from Mycenae, artisans from our inland towns, farmers from the west. Each group had their heads together, speaking softly, darting their eyes about. But each time one of them saw me, he gave warning and the others stopped their talk and stood silent, until I'd passed and was out of earshot. I was ready to give up when Andrios said I'd never find out anything as long as I walked about as Drupos the Boxer. So I borrowed a potter's smock from a friend in the Palace workshops and got one of the Egyptian tumblers to show me how to alter my face, for they are past masters at that art. Then I went back to the market place at Amnisos."

He stopped to take a breath, and Thalamika asked, "Have you found out anything?"

"Not enough. But a little. They are careful in what they say and give little away even when they feel safe with one of their own kind. I pretended I'd just come to Amnisos. I sat in a winehouse looking, I hope, lost and forlorn until another potter came and spoke to me. I offered him wine, saying I'd made—thanks to The Goddess who'd sent me a sign—a lucky sale of many cups and vases and would like to celebrate with one of my trade. He wasn't slow to help me, and I saw to it his wine was strong while mine was well watered."

If the situation hadn't been so serious, Thalamika could have laughed at Drupos. He was so obviously proud of his skill as an actor, proud that he'd fooled her so completely with his false face.

"When my friend's wits were a little muddled," he went on, "I began to question him, but muddled or not I could draw nothing but hints from him."

"What hints? What did he *say*, Drupos?"

"*Will* you let me tell this in my own way, Thalamika? Be quiet and listen or I shan't tell it at all. It took time to get what little I did from the real potter, and that came in fragments between long, rambling accounts of his own woes and frequent curses called down upon the Priest-King who, he said, was ruining all the artisans in Crete, not to mention the farmers with his overlasting taxes. But, in the end, I gathered there's to be some kind of uprising, though when and where I couldn't find out. This man comes from near the ruins of Gournia, and it may be this is no more than part of the general trouble over taxes we already know of. But he did speak one thing clearly.

When I pressed him a little for details, saying—may The Goddess forgive me—I would, myself, like to join this conspiracy, he shook his finger at me, solemn as an owl though by then he could hardly sit on his stool for drunkenness, and said, 'Don't ask me, friend potter. I'm sworn to say nothing and no amount of your good wine (here he half-rose from his chair and made me a silly, lopsided bow) will make me foreswear myself. The penalty would be a knife in my back, and then where would my wife and my twelve little children be? So don't ask me. Ask the one who knows. Ask Myrtis. Ask the Queen. *She* knows!' And then he folded his arms upon the table and put his head on them and began such a snorting and snoring he sounded like a wild boar. I knew he'd talk no more and left him."

Thalamika drew in her breath. "The Queen!" she said. "I'm not surprised. I've never trusted that woman. But, Drupos, did your potter say anything about Kretheus?"

"No," Drupos said, "but I'll tell you one thing I'm sure of. The Mycenean merchants are in the middle of this somehow. They go about the port in pairs or groups, never alone now. When they knew me as Drupos they scowled and avoided me, but yesterday, disguised as I was, they didn't know me. So I managed to get quite near two who were talking softly beside a clothseller's booth. One of them said, 'Hush' and looked at me hard, and the other said, 'You're right, though he's likely safe enough being a potter.' But they talked of other things while I stood near them, and I didn't dare stay close too long for fear they'd suspect me of spying and call the Guardians of the Peace."

Thalamika said, "And now, Andrios?"

He answered slowly as if he didn't like the shape of the words and would keep them within his head if he could. "The time is here, as I knew it would be."

"To tell Minos of the Queen?"

"To tell Minos. Though I'm ready to swear it will do no good. Still, he must be told. I must, at least, try to warn him. Poseidon!" He drove one fist into the palm of the other hand. "I wish it weren't I who must face him with his people's plots and his Queen's treachery. As I was saying to Drupos when you came rushing to my rescue, if he believes me it will break his heart and if he doesn't he'll likely have my life. Still it's got to be done and there's no one else but me to do it."

CHAPTER
TWELVE

Thalamika swung her feet over the side of her tumbled bed and groped her way in the night-filled room to a chest near the door. She found a small lamp and took it to the hall and lit it from the night light on the wall and went back into her room. She wouldn't try to sleep any longer. Her bed was ample token, if she needed a token, that the night had been wasted. If she'd slept at all, and she didn't think she had, she'd done no more than doze now and then and each time started up at once, wondering how Andrios had fared with the Priest-King.

They had decided last night in the grove not to meet again after Andrios had seen Minos. It would be late; whatever happened would happen and news of it could wait until morning. They'd agreed Thalamika should go home to the evening meal and then to sleep. Drupos would return to the port to wait and watch. They would meet after the Procession of the Sacred Vessels to hear what had happened.

So they had decided and Drupos had gone off alone into the dark-gathering night. Thalamika had walked with Andrios to a little gate in the Palace wall. They hadn't spoken, for each felt there was nothing left to be said, but their silence had been friendly and comfortable. Thalamika had put her hand on Andrios' arm and he had covered it lightly with his, and she'd felt warm and secure and almost happy in spite of nagging uncertainty about the future of their country.

They had bade one another good night, briefly and gravely, and she'd prayed in her heart that The Goddess would bless his meeting with Minos and had gone home quickly, thinking of food and bed.

But she hadn't slept, and now in the blackest hour of the night, the hour before the first gray forerunner of the dawn spread ghostlike up from the horizon, she couldn't stay in her bed or her room any longer. She'd dress, she thought, and go quietly through the house and out into the garden. Perhaps the dawn-released fragrance of the flowers and herbs, the dawn-greeting song of birds would bring her a measure of rest.

She eased the house door open. It made no sound, and she left it ajar so the clicking of the latch wouldn't disturb the sleep of those fortunate enough to have found it. A light mist shrouded the garden, and before her eyes became accustomed to it she stumbled against a stone seat and jumped back, terror catching in her throat. She put out her hand and felt along the surface of the bench, and knew it for what it was and laughed a little shakily at herself. She found the pebbled path and walked along it, breathing in the soft, sweet odors of night-blooming plants; the tangy-sharp fragrance of mint and thyme, dittany and parsley. A nightingale poured out upon the quiet garden his last paean to the dark and was still. An owl hooted once softly nearby. There were hidden rustlings and small grumblings in the borders along the path. The night creatures, she thought, were settling down against the coming day into their safe nests and burrows and tree holes.

She sighed, feeling tension and worry go slowly from her muscles and mind. She'd walk to the end of the garden. There she could see the House of the Priest-King, and she'd offer her morning prayers to The Goddess as the sun touched the Horns of Consecration above the South Gate. She found herself thinking about Andrios, and unaccountably wishing he were here with her, and she felt surprise at herself, for she'd never wished to be with him without some specific reason before.

She stood waiting in the stillness of the predawn, watching the stars go out one by one as the milky white promise of another day spread upward from the edge of the sky. In a few minutes the white would turn to gold and rose when the returning sun touched it, and she prepared in her mind her salutation to the Lady of the Air who would send her light for another day over the waiting world.

She never made the salutation. She didn't see the sun gild the Horns of Consecration. In that breath-holding moment between night and day the stillness was driven out of the garden by a branch that cracked beneath a step, by a breath expelled in a long sigh. She whirled around and saw Andrios. There was a red welt across one cheek. His eyes held a hurt look and his hands were shaking a little as he held them out to her. "Thank The Goddess you're here, Thalamika. I've been waiting an hour hidden behind the wall, hoping, but not really daring to hope, you'd come out. I . . ." He stopped and made a small, vague gesture with his shoulders as if he were too tired or too hopeless to go on.

She touched the long mark and felt it crusted with dried blood and knew a sudden fierce tenderness for him that came unbidden and unexpected, and anger at the person who had done this to him. "What is it, Andrios?" she asked. "What's happened to you?"

His throat moved as he tried to answer her, but he couldn't sound the words. He stood, drooping, wracked by some inner misery, and looked at her as if he had lost his very soul. Pity for him grew in her heart and mind and exploded into something else she didn't at first recognize, though it rocked and buffeted her. "Andrios!" she said and took his face in her hands and kissed him. "Andrios, my dear!"

For one amazed second he looked at her, still limp with his own misery. Then, like a flower long parched for water that revives with the benison of rain, his body straightened and tightened and his eyes that had been glazed and dull with suffering began to dance with joy. He cried her name gladly and put his arms around her and kissed her greedily, as if he would spend at once all the long pent emotion of his love. They stood so until a woodlark began his morning song and Andrios kissed her once again and set her gently away from him, and they looked at one another having no words for what was in their hearts nor any need for words.

Another bird and another joined the woodlark until the whole garden seemed to be singing. Andrios took her hand and led her to the bench, and some of the hurt look came back into his eyes. He stood looking down at her as she sat with the dawnlight reflecting upon water drops left in her hair by the withdrawing mist. Then he sat beside her and started to put his arm around her and did not and said aloud, "I mustn't. Not now. There's no *time*." She touched the red mark again and said, "Who did this to you, my Andrios?"

"It's nothing, Thalamika. It will go away and it doesn't hurt much now. It's my heart that hurts. Minos gave me the mark."

She said, "Minos!" and knew she'd been in danger of forgetting everything except the stunning realization of her love for Andrios. So his talk with the Priest-King hadn't gone well. "Tell me," she said.

"At first he listened patiently enough to all I said, but when I came to the meat of what Drupos told us he began to scowl and got up from his throne and walked about the room. His face got redder and redder and I knew he was angry, but he listened still until I'd told him everything except the accusation of the Queen. Though I knew I must go on I was, I confess it, frightened and I stopped to find courage. When I paused he shouted at me, calling me a timid fool finding trouble where none existed even it had to be in the wandering thoughts of a drunken potter. He said again that without a fleet the Myceneans would dare nothing and that he, Minos, must have time to prepare his people. He said he'd not thought I, chosen for special training by the Priest-King himself, would so doubt his decisions or question the judgment of my master. If there were serious disaffection among his people, he would be the first to know, not a youngster who'd seen his first Bull Games a bare seven years ago. Then he paused and took breath, and I reminded him he'd asked me to act the spy. He said I was bringing him nothing new but the same old rumors and asked scornfully why, if we were so sure of plots, Drupos the Boxer had not discovered the time and place set for this fancied uprising. Then, Thalamika, then I told him what Drupos had heard of the Queen."

Andrios drew in his breath sharply, remembering the Priest-King's anger, and the sound, as much as anything he'd said, brought Thalamika entirely and finally out of her golden haze of love to a full realization of all he'd been saying. She was frightened and to give herself courage she took his hand and held it tightly and said, "What did he do then?"

"Then," the words came out slowly as if they hurt him, "then his face went white and his whole body trembled and he looked at me with such a look of hatred as I've never seen in him before, and he rushed at me and drove his fist at my face. I turned my head a little as he came so his blow didn't land as he'd intended, upon my temple—for I believe he meant to kill me if he could. But the great amethyst ring with the seal of his office raked my cheek and, seeing the blood flow, he stepped back and stared and didn't try again to strike me. His face was livid and his breath came in hard gasps and I was afraid he'd fall into a fit. I didn't dare make a sound or move, and he stood before me panting a full minute before he could speak again."

Andrios put his hands over his face as if he would shut out the memory of his uncle's hatred. Thalamika thought her heart would break at his agony, but she knew he was beyond any human comforting and held herself quiet beside him, waiting until he could go on. She felt the shudder that shook his whole body, felt him grow still after it, and relaxed as he relaxed at last slowly.

"When Minos finally spoke again, I could hardly hear him, for his voice was whisper-low and hoarse and the words came strangled from his throat. He said, 'I should have you stoned, liar and bearer of false witness. But you are of my house and I would not make your evil thoughts known to my people. I don't know why you seek to poison my mind with this tale of my Queen's treachery. She's good and loyal and just, the mother of my well-loved son and my own true wife. She would do nothing to harm me or my kingdom. But I do know this. I do not want to see your face again, or hear your voice. And this I command. Go from me and from my lands. Now. And come no more before me if you wish to live.'"

Andrios had spoken more and more softly. His words faded at the end so she could scarcely hear them. She wondered if she *had* heard and she said, "No, Andrios. Not—banishment!" and he said, "Yes," and nothing more, only looked at her with eyes so sad they hurt her.

"You will go?"

He raised his head which had been hidden again in his hands and looked out over the garden toward the towers of the Palace and stayed so for long seconds. A swarm of bees, a black mass flying down a shaft of light from the risen sun, came across the wall. Their droning was loud in the morning, and Andrios' eyes followed them. When each busy creature had found a flower and was sucking its nectar to take back to the stored honeycomb, he straightened his body on the bench and turned to her and took her face in his hands and smiled a little bleakly.

"How can I, Thalamika, when I've at last found my lady and my heart's desire?"

She could hardly breathe, caught between love of him and fear for his safety. "He'll kill you!" she cried. "Andrios, he'll surely kill you if he finds you here. You must go. Now. At once. There's a ship which will sail this day for Melos. Drupos told me. He knows the Captain. I'll come later when . . ."

He put his hand gently over her mouth to stop her. "Would you really have me go and leave you whom I love better than my life and this loved land surely threatened by unknown danger? No, Thalamika, I shall not go. But don't be afraid for me. Minos won't find me and, if The Goddess and Poseidon will help me, I'll save him and his people in spite of his blindness."

"But, Andrios . . ."

"Listen, Thalamika. Do you know the cave in the hillside above the House of the Priestess, the cave, men say, where those who came before us worshiped their gods?"

"Yes."

"I'll go there as soon as the Procession begins when all the people of the Palace and the towns are lining the Sacred Way. Minos will head the Procession and I'll go over the fields, in a plain cloak and with my head covered, so even if I'm seen no one will recognize me. The cave will be my hiding place at need. More important, it will be a place where you can leave a sign if you want me."

"What sign?" Only by pretending she was listening to a story about other people could she keep herself from crying out in despair.

"Lay two twigs crossed so." He broke two bits from a fallen branch and laid them crosswise. "If you or Drupos have news I should hear, leave only the sticks. I'll find you or find a way to get word to you. But if there's some immediate danger, place a pebble in the middle of the sticks. So."

She nodded to show she understood and said, "You'll need food, Andrios, and wine and fire. The nights are cold in the mountains."

"Food, yes," he said. "I'll do without wine. There's a spring of sweet water nearby. It wouldn't be safe to show fire, but I'll take my winter cloak and it will keep me warm enough." He smiled a little at her concern for his needs. "Besides, my Thalamika, I'll not stay in the cave. It won't be any more than a lair to be used when I need it by day and a place to shelter at night. I'll be going about, adding my eyes and ears to yours and Drupos'. And remember, I've friends in the hills. If I learn anything, I'll get word to you. Can Chryses be trusted?"

"Yes. If I tell her we are afraid the Myceneans are trying to harm us. She hates them all, because of those who enslaved her and her people."

"Good," he said.

Behind them a door was closed and he stood up. "I shouldn't be found here, Thalamika, and the household's stirring. Can you bring the food and hide it beneath the bench where the thyme grows thickest? I'll come for it when the Procession has started and the house is empty."

She'd gotten up when he did and stood beside him, looking and feeling as if she were about to lose the world and all her happiness. He took her in his arms and held her, whispering into her ear until she stopped trembling. Then he kissed her once and dropped his arms and said, "Go quickly, Thalamika, and don't be afraid. The Goddess will protect us. We'll be separated a little while, but when this is over, there'll be no more separation for us—ever."

She didn't believe him, didn't think he believed himself. She wanted to cry out that she wouldn't leave him, wanted to beg him to take her, too, to the cave, but she forced back the plea, knowing what his answer would be, not wanting to add another burden to his already heavy heart. She touched his wounded cheek once more and said, "Stay safe," and turned away before he should see her tears, and ran to the house door.

She could hear voices and bustlings in the house as the slaves made ready for the day, but no one saw her come in and she went up the stairs and to her room without meeting anyone. She wanted to throw herself upon her tumbled bed and weep until she had spent all her tears, but she knew she hadn't time for such indulgence. Her dress was draggled with dew and she took it off, pushing it out of sight at the bottom of her chest. She'd have to get it out later and send it to the fuller—the fuller in Amnisos, not the one in the Palace who would be curious about how the Lady Thalamika came to have wet clothes when the weather had been fine for so many days. She wanted no one speculating about her, for such speculations might prove a danger to Andrios.

She must hurry. As a Priestess she must take her place in the Procession of the Sacred Vessels, no matter what her desolation of spirit. Where was her ceremonial skirt? Where was Chryses? She should have been here by now.

Thalamika went to the door to call the slave and met Chryses coming in. "Zeus keep you safe this day, Mistress," the slave said, and Thalamika returned the salutation, not knowing she did so. "Where *is* my skirt? Find it, Chryses. And please hurry."

"There's time, O Mistress," Chryses said in a flat voice as she handed her the long skirt, made to look like a panther's skin, which Priestesses had worn on ritual occasions since a time beyond man's memory.

Thalamika's hands were shaking so she couldn't adjust the skirt, and she said, "Help me, Chryses."

Chryses looked at her curiously but she made no comment. She draped the skirt and fastened it before she said, "The lamp in the room of the Lady Philona was shrouded in red last night, O Mistress."

"Now hand me my . . . WHAT? What did you say, Chryses?"

"The Lady Philona's light showed red when I went last night to watch for the signal."

Thalamika sat down upon the bed, staring at Chryses. "You are sure?"

"I'm sure," the slave said. "I hid in the garden of the House of Phelleus before nightfall as was my custom and I saw the lamp lighted, and a little later the light turned from white to red."

"Why didn't you come and tell me at once?"

"I couldn't, O Mistress." Chryses kept her voice expressionless, trying to keep from her mind the remembrance of fright-filled hours. "I waited where I was for a little to be certain it *was* the signal and not some mistake. When the red shroud remained I started to leave the garden. But I had waited too long. I found the gate in the wall barred and guarded, and I couldn't come away without being discovered and questioned. I didn't want to bring trouble to the Lady Philona or to you, O Mistress, so I went back to my hiding place and waited until sunrise when the guard opened the gate and went away."

Thalamika stared at her slave, thinking of the long, chill hours which must have been full of terrors for this Attic woman who feared the dark as she feared death and believed it full of evil spirits. She went and put her arms about Chryses, seeing her for the first time not as a slave but as a woman not much older than herself. "Thank you, Chryses," she said. "It must have been hard."

Chryses blinked her eyes to keep back the tears. "Nothing is too hard if it will bring harm to the Myceneans," she said, and Thalamika told her, then, of Andrios' plans. "Will you help us, Chryses?" she finished.

Chryses nodded though her face wore a troubled look, and Thalamika told her to be always on the watch for a message from Andrios and, if it came, bring it quickly to her. She hugged Chryses again and said, "When this is over you shall have your freedom, for you've been more friend to me than slave, though I've only just realized it."

Chryses' tears spilled over then but all she said was, "Thank you, O Mistress. Now I'd better go and prepare a packet of food for the Lord Andrios. I'll leave it beneath the bench among the thyme and watch to see he gets it unobserved." She didn't look at Thalamika again as she hurried out of the door and Thalamika let her go, knowing she would be better alone.

Thalamika stood where she was, plucking at her lip. What could she do about the signal? She couldn't stay away from the Procession or leave it before the end. Her duties as Priestess would keep her from the market place until long past the time when she should meet Philona's messenger as they had planned. And there was no time to look for Drupos even if she knew where to look. She didn't even know whether he was in Knossos or Amnisos. She would have to go herself, when the day was over, to the garden of the House of Phelleus and trust to The Goddess to show her some way of getting Philona's attention.

Poor Philona. What would she think when her servant returned with word that Thalamika hadn't come to the meeting place? Why did this have to happen today? Her thoughts were whirling and her head buzzing like the bees in the garden. She mustn't stand here. Her legs, her whole body, felt as heavy as if she'd been cast in bronze, but she made an effort and forced herself to leave the warm protection of her room.

CHAPTER
THIRTEEN

The Sacred Way stretched, white under the sun, ahead
of the line of young men and women carrying rhytons of
gold and steatite, some carved in the likeness of a bull's
head, others funnel-shaped; libation jugs of fine pottery,
richly decorated with realistic designs from nature; fig-
urines of votaries, arms snake-wreathed; two-edged bronze
axes of all sizes; the golden bull mask the Priest-King
would wear when he sacrificed the bull tomorrow to the
Earth Mother and Poseidon—all the cult objects used in
worshiping The Goddess and kept in hidden storehouses
in the House of the Priest-King, except when they were
used at the festivals or shown to the people on special
occasions such as this. Colors seemed to dance in the clear,
bright air as the Procession moved slowly, to the music
of pipes, between tight-packed rows of men and women
—artisans, merchants, sailors, slaves from the town;
farmers and herders, from the countryside; charcoal burners and woodcutters from the mountains. They had pushed
and crowded for the best places but now they were
quiet, watching in awe. Minos headed the Procession,
holding before him a small gold Labrys, a replica of the
big bronze double axes. He wore a long, one-piece gown,

white, bordered in blue, that covered him from neck to feet. His hair was bound with a gold fillet set with precious stones, flashing and winking as the sun caught them. He held himself straight, as if he would stand taller than his short stature, and kept his eyes set ahead so no one could see them. Thalamika had seen them when he passed close to her to take his place. They were clouded with pain and anger, and she thought he was suffering and she was glad. She thought, too, he looked ill. His face was mottled red and white and beaded with sweat, and he walked slowly and seemed to find it hard to breathe. But when the Procession started, he summoned some hidden control and moved with his usual dignity and grace. The Young Prince, wearing kilts for the first time instead of his boy's smock, walked behind him and was followed by the Chief Counselors and the bearers of the ritual vessels in the skinlike skirts which marked them as votaries of The Goddess.

The Procession moved slowly along the Sacred Way. There could be no hurry. Every person who made up the crowd must be given time to see each rhyton and mask and ax and reverence it. Thalamika thought the whole of Crete must be watching. She had a curious sense that, for this day, time was standing still; that the fields had ceased to grow and the flocks had fallen into a trance while the men and women who tended them came to Knossos to find a blessing in the sight of the altar furnishings of the Lady of the Labyrinth. She knew this wasn't true. Other men and women, thousands of them, tended flocks and crops, spun wool into thread and dyed it and wove it into cloth; stood by the cooking fires and sailed the ships and burned charcoal and felled the trees for the shipbuilders and did all the other things needed to keep their lives and their land in accustomed ways. But the feeling of timelessness continued, and she couldn't rid herself of it until, at last, she ceased to think or feel and put one foot before the other without knowing she did so.

She wondered, later that afternoon as she went in the sunset down the long hill to Amnisos, what had come over her during those hours when her spirit and body seemed to be separated. She remembered another time when such a thing had happened to her, at Phaistos when she was still a child. She had been caught in some wickedness she could no longer recall and had been scolded by her father, who seldom raised his voice to her. He had been stern that day, and when she'd tried to wheedle him into gentleness and laughter he had frowned and sent her away, telling her to think about her sins and pray The Goddess to keep her from such mischief. She had been angry and hurt and had run from him and out to the hills that surrounded the Palace and sat upon a rock and watched the sky above Mount Ida. But gradually she'd been possessed by something to which she couldn't put a name and by this same sense of timelessness, this same feeling that her spirit floated somewhere separate from her body set apart from her world. She had felt as if she were no longer one with ordinary living but was, instead, a part of the rock and the ground beneath it and the red and blue flowers at her feet and the vast sky above her. And, as she had sat there, she had seen an olive grove hanging in the air, high above the mountain, and huge shapes of men stalking across the sky. And, strangely, she hadn't been afraid.

The olive trees and the shadows of giant men had disappeared, leaving only the well-known mountain and the rocks and flowers and, far off, a glimpse of the sea where the mountain broke in two and fell abruptly to the shoreline. She'd gone to find her mother and tell what she'd seen. The Lady Kalmia had held her close and kissed her and said she'd been given a sign by the Lady of the Skies, and from that day she'd been vowed to serve The Goddess and taught by the Chief Priestess at Phaistos those things most seemly to a votary of the Earth Mother.

She'd never questioned her mother's words. She didn't, really, question them now. Puzzling over today's experience, she decided it was not the same thing. She'd learned to know, in the years between, the signs that meant The Goddess possessed her mind, and such signs had been absent today. She wondered if what had occurred to her today hadn't rather been caused by lack of sleep and food, for she'd forgotten her morning meal; by the sudden realization of her love for Andrios which must have been growing, unrecognized, until knowledge of it was released when she saw him so hurt in spirit and flesh; and by her fear for his safety.

Whatever the cause, the separateness was gone now and she was one again. Chryses had seen to that when her mistress had come, like a sleepwalker, home from the Procession. Chryses had brought food, and milk in a thin, glazed cup, and forced her to eat. Chryses had made her lie down and she had slept, deeply, without dreams, until the afternoon was far spent. And while she slept Chryses had looked for Drupos in the Palace and in the towns of Knossos and Amnisos.

But Drupos couldn't be found, and Thalamika wouldn't

send for Andrios as Chryses urged her to do. If she went to the cave and placed the signal, he would, as soon as he found it, come to the garden. She knew this, knew it as if she were inside his mind. And she knew that if he were seen or Minos heard of it, he would surely be taken and killed. She would, she'd decided, go herself to the House of Phelleus and find some way of talking to Philona.

She was none too soon. The gate was open and un-guarded still, but as she slid through it and hid herself behind a statue of the Mycenean god Apollo she could hear the talk of two guards coming along the path toward the gate. She didn't dare move until the gate banged shut. Then she crept from her hiding place and went shadow-like through the falling dark to a spot from which she could see the whole side of the tall house. It loomed above her, five stories high, and she watched it while, one by one, the oiled parchment that filled the window frames blossomed with the soft yellow flowers of lighted lamps. She guessed Philona would be prisoned somewhere near the top of the house, and she hoped her friend would be wise enough to show the red signal again. She'd been a fool to forget to ask Chryses the location of Philona's room.

She counted her heartbeats while the top stories remained dark. She didn't know how she was going to talk to Philona. Unless the signal came she had no chance at all, because without it she'd have no idea where to find the captive. She looked with dark-accustomed eyes about the garden, hoping to find a ladder that might reach to the top of the house. There was none in sight, but she guessed there must be some way of getting to the roof in order to replace the red tiles that covered it. She would have to search further and so increase the danger of discovery.

She looked again and saw the red signal and almost fainted with relief that at least she knew where Philona was. She started slowly, cautiously, as quietly as a wild boar who knows the hunters have discovered his lair, to look for the ladder.

She stopped and listened and heard nothing in the night except an occasional clink as the guards shifted their position. Yet she was uneasy. The very stillness seemed danger-filled. The hairs on her arms stood up straight and the back of her neck crawled. She took two more careful steps toward the dark blur in the corner she thought was the gardener's shed. She still had heard nothing when a hand covered her mouth and an arm circled her waist, holding her helpless. She couldn't move her head but she could see out of the corner of her eyes a long-healed scar on a face that seemed mountain-high above her, and knew herself captured by the giant slave of Phelleus before fear filled her and robbed her of consciousness.

When she was aware again of herself, she was lying upon a kind of shelf barely covered with a worn sheepskin. By a single small, rough-made lamp, she could make out a boxlike room, almost bare of furnishings. She thought she was likely in the room of the slave and alone, for she neither saw another form in the shadows, nor heard any sound of breathing. She moaned softly, cursing her own stupidity in coming here alone.

As if the moan had been an incantation, the figure of a woman appeared, conjured from the shadows. Before Thalamika could cry out the fear and awe in her mind, the woman put a cautioning finger to her own lips and knelt on the earthen floor and whispered, "Don't be afraid, Lady Thalamika. You are safe and no one means you harm. My husband only wanted to be sure you didn't cry out in the garden. He didn't mean to frighten you. I'll go now and get him."

She got up in one quick, graceful movement and Thalamika saw she was tall and fair-haired, dressed in the fashion of the mainland in a wide, flowing gown of some dark stuff belted at the waist with a simple, twisted cord. Her bare feet made no sound as she went toward the door, and her breath came so softly it couldn't be heard two paces from the place where Thalamika lay. The stranger eased open the door and closed it gently behind her.

Thalamika sat up at once. This was her opportunity to escape, for, in spite of the woman's gentle-voiced assurances, she felt herself trapped and prisoned. The woman must have forgotten to shoot home the outside bolt, for there had been no sound. I must hurry, Thalamika thought, and fought against a dizziness in her head. She forced herself to get off the shelf and she was half-way across the room before she stopped.

Where were her wits? What good to leave this room when she had no idea where she was; when, even if she could find her way in time to the garden, she couldn't leave it because of the guard? Better to stay here, at least until daylight. The room, since it was earth-floored, must be at ground level. She could make out, even in the dim light, the square that showed a window. By daylight she could manage somehow to cut away its parchment—with an edge of her bracelet or the sealstone hung about her neck—and crawl out and run.

She sensed, rather than heard, the cautious opening

of the door and went quickly back to the shelf. She had just time enough to sit upon it, hoping her face was more composed than her mind, before the woman came in again followed by the big slave with the scarred face. He came to her quickly, moving almost silently in spite of his size, and bowed low before her. She fought the terror that wanted to break into a scream and made herself think of Andrios. The thought steadied her and, out of the steadying, came memory of Andrios by the shore telling of this slave, of his gentleness and his past life when he lived a free man in Troy and was an actor in the theater there.

She looked at him then, standing tall above her and quiet, as if he would give her time to get used to his presence before he spoke, and she managed a little smile. He bowed again and knelt, as the woman had done, beside her and spoke softly.

"Thank you, O Lady Thalamika, for that smile. It gives me courage to beg you to hear me and give me your trust, for without it I can do nothing for you."

She saw his eyes, calm and steady. They were kind eyes and his voice was kind. Dear Andrios. He'd been right. She wondered how he had come to know so much about this man.

"I'll trust you," she said, "for Andrios has told me you are highborn and gentle."

"I thank the Lord Andrios," he said and made a gesture into the room. The woman came to stand near them and the man went on. "I am Glaucus," he said and she heard pride in the words, "and this is my wife, Turitis. We are, or were until today, slaves of Phelleus." The voice hardened in bitterness.

Thalamika moved restlessly. She was impatient at the deliberate speech and wished he would tell her what was happening and leave the introductions until later. Turitis guessed her thoughts or read them and said, "Patience, O Lady Thalamika. There's time enough, and it's better for you to hear our story first. Glaucus," she smiled at him affectionately, "must tell it in his own way."

Thalamika nodded and Glaucus went on. "We've been slaves in this household for ten years, since a band of raiders from the north came in the night to Troy and stole our goods and burned our houses and took us away and sold us in the slave market at Athens. We tried to fight but we were a peaceful people, unaccustomed to weapons, and the raiders surprised us in our sleep. An agent of Phelleus bought us to be house slaves and we've lived here since, if the existence of a slave can be called living. And through all those years we've hoarded what little we could of gifts or goods discarded as unworthy by Phelleus, but salable nevertheless for a pittance in the market place, against the time when we could go to the magistrate and pay the price of our freedom. But that time seemed far away until your cousin Drupos, by his gift to Turitis in return for talk with the Lady Philona, made our freedom good and today we went, when Phelleus was at the shore seeing to his ships, and bought ourselves clear and received proof of it." He took a small roll of parchment from the belt of his plain Mycenean tunic and showed her the magistrate's seal.

"Then why are you still here in the House of Phelleus?" Thalamika asked, puzzled that free people would still pretend to be slaves.

Glaucus sat back on his heels and looked at her, and

his face was transformed by some inner magic into that of a stern judge. "We have no love for Phelleus, O Lady Thalamika. He wronged us and he must pay our price. Three times in these ten years he promised us our freedom in return for special service of a burdensome or dangerous kind, and three times, once the service was done, he denied his word. Turitis has, besides, become fond of the gentle Lady Philona. So we will, at once, return wrong for wrong and help the Lady Philona and Drupos the Boxer. He couldn't come to the garden tonight, so I waited for you to tell you of our plans."

"*Waited* for me? But—but how did you know I'd come?"

"An hour ago someone brushed past me as I walked in the market place and slipped a note into my hand. The note said only that you would be in the garden at nightfall. It was signed Chryses."

How had Chryses known to send him word, Thalamika wondered, and gave up trying to find the answer and said, "I don't understand. You spoke of plans. What plans? And why does the Lady Philona need help now?"

Glaucus started to answer her questions in reverse order. "Tomorrow," he said, "before the sun is up, Phelleus will send the Lady Philona out of Amnisos to his villa in the hills. I haven't been able to learn his reasons for sending her now, for I've been often, these last days, upon errands that have kept me from the house. But she will go, for Phelleus has ordered Turitis and me to accompany her. Once he has her safely hidden he will, I'm sure, take her secretly to Mycenae, for he has lost hope she'll ever deny her mother's land and people."

"We must get word to Drupos," Thalamika put in

quickly. "He'd never forgive me if I didn't warn him. Do you know where he is?"

"No, my lady, but he'll be ready tomorrow. He knows the plan and he'll rescue the Lady Philona before she's gone far upon the road. He wanted me to tell you to meet him in the garden of his father's house an hour after midnight with food for three days and your warmest cloak for the Lady Philona. Turitis doesn't dare tell her old nurse to pack a warm cloak, in case Phelleus should decide to examine her belongings and become suspicious at finding clothes for the season of storms among them. And Drupos the Boxer asks you to tell my Lord Andrios to join you there in the garden."

Thalamika's face showed how disturbed she was. "But, Glaucus," she said, "hadn't you heard? Andrios—Andrios has been banished by Minos."

"Banished! Poseidon help us now! Has the Lord Andrios left the island already?"

"No. But he's well hidden in the hills."

"Where?"

"I don't know where he is at this moment, but I know how to get word to him. But, Glaucus, he mustn't be seen in Knossos or Amnisos. If Minos knows he's still . . ."

"Yes. Yes." Glaucus' forehead was pushed into a net of wrinkles. "What can we do then?" He waited, thinking, and asked, "How would you get word to him?"

Thalamika didn't answer. Did she dare trust this man with her knowledge of the cave? She'd not even told Chryses yet. Glaucus said impatiently, "Come, Lady Thalamika. You promised to trust me. Would I have gone so far if I had intended to deal falsely with you? I'd do nothing to bring harm to the Lord Andrios. He was only a boy when I came to Amnisos, but when I saw him first in the market place he didn't taunt me for my slavery and my battered face as the other boys did, but greeted me gravely and courteously. Later he sought me out and took delight in stories of my country and begged me to teach him the art of acting. He's my friend. Now, if you know where he can be found, tell me. It may not be necessary for me to know. But it could be important. I'm not sure what's in Drupos' mind, but I think he wants my Lord Andrios to talk to the Lady Philona as soon as possible."

She told him then of the way to the cave, and he nodded. "If anything should go wrong, I'll find my way to the Lord Andrios and tell him what I know."

He rose to his feet and stretched his hand to Thalamika. "Now come," he said. "It's already late and you must sleep awhile before you meet Drupos the Boxer."

She went with him, and he led her by a dark and winding passage out of the House of Phelleus and through a hidden gate in the garden wall, well away from the guard, and by silent back streets in Amnisos and Knossos to her aunt's house.

CHAPTER
FOURTEEN

"Drupos?" Thalamika's whisper scarcely disturbed the dark, but Drupos must have been expecting it, for he said as softly, "Here, Thalamika," and came and took her arm. "Come to the end of the garden where there'll be no chance of a wakeful slave hearing us."

She went with him, thinking love and fear for Philona had taught him caution.

"Now," he said when he judged them a safe distance from the house, "did you bring the food and the warm cloak for Philona?"

"Yes, and a cloak for myself. I'm going with you, Drupos."

"NO! Thalamika. There may be danger, possibly even a fight."

"I'm going, Drupos. There are things you don't know yet, so listen to me and don't argue. Andrios has been banished the kingdom by Minos"—Drupos drew in his breath, gasping as if he'd taken an unexpected blow—"for speaking against the Queen. He's left Knossos but not the kingdom. He's hiding in the hills above the House of the Priestess, trying to find out more of what's happening in the kingdom. We must take Philona there, and may

The Goddess grant she'll have something to tell Andrios."

"Do you know where he'll be? Can we surely find him?"

"I don't know exactly, but that's a chance we'll have to take. I think he'll come to a cave I know of to sleep. If we don't find him, I'll leave a signal we arranged for. How are you planning to rescue Philona?"

He wished his mind worked as quickly as hers. He was full of questions about Andrios, but he thought they'd have to wait until later. He couldn't yet see how much Andrios' absence would affect their plans. He wished he knew more of what Philona knew. He shook his head and kept his mind to the main business of her rescue. "Glaucus says she's to be taken while it's still dark on the road to Phaistos, which leads also to the summer villa of Phelleus. Glaucus will be among the men set to guard her and Turitis will be with her. Spyros and three other boxers will come out of an olive grove just where the road bends south. They'll be dressed as farmers and each will drive an ass loaded with fodder." He paused to chuckle briefly, thinking of the little beasts. "You know what a nuisance loaded asses can be on the road, Thalamika, with fodder so thick on each side the small creatures are broader than they're long and so bulky and awkward they can't move quickly. Spyros and the others will drive the asses among the slaves of Phelleus and make a great noise of shouting and cursing meanwhile to confuse the escort, who won't be expecting that kind of trouble before daylight. Philona will be riding in a covered cart and Glaucus and Turitis will lead it out of the confusion, back toward Knossos, where I'll be waiting to take her into the hills."

"*We'll* be waiting, Drupos, and we'll take her straight to Andrios."

He said no again, but he knew it was useless to argue with her. Besides he'd like to have her with him because he was too confused by all the changes to think really straight. She paid no attention to his refusal and went on. "What of Glaucus and Turitis? And Spyros and his friends?"

"Spyros will keep the escort occupied long enough for Glaucus and Turitis to lose themselves in the dark. I've made arrangements with one of my father's ship captains to take them on his ship, which is leaving today for the islands. He'll see them safely home to Troy. As to my friends," he laughed softly, "have no fear for them. When their task is done, they'll be off before the escort knows what's happened."

Thalamika nodded, forgetting that in the dark garden Drupos couldn't see her. She wished she had time to get a valuable gift for Glaucus and Turitis, something they could barter in Troy for things they'd need to start their new life. Too late for that now. But no doubt her uncle would send other trading ships, and one of his captains would carry a gift for her.

Drupos had his head on one side, listening. From near the gate into the garden came the hoarse sound of a frog croaking, and Drupos said, "Come then, if you must. Spyros is ready at the gate and it's time to be off."

The rescue took place just as Drupos planned. Philona, shaking but happy, climbed down from the cart and stood a moment in Drupos' arms. There was no time for explanations. They said a hurried farewell to Glaucus and

Turitis and saw them lose themselves in a grove by the road. The boxers were still shouting and the escort running about when Thalamika led Drupos and Philona onto a hill path she'd walked with Kretheus and knew to be the shortest route to Andrios. She'd taken charge because Drupos and Philona seemed unable to do anything except look at one another as if they'd drunk a love philter. They seemed to have no need to talk, and Thalamika hustled them away from the road, knowing they must reach the cave while it was still dark.

A late sliver of moon was just sinking, and in the east the morning star glowed yellow, standing out clearly among the hosts of other, lesser stars. The waning moon and the stars lighted the path so the three of them could walk it quickly without stumbling. Thalamika felt as if they were the last three people left in a lonely dark world and shivered and quickened her pace.

Half an hour's walk brought them to the cave, and Thalamika called into its darkness, "Andrios!"

No sound came from the black entrance and she began to fear he hadn't come back here to sleep and to her dread for him was added worry about Philona. Then she heard a rustling in the yellow-flowered shrubs above them and a cautious whisper, "Thalamika, is it you?"

"Yes. And Drupos and Philona. Come down quickly, Andrios."

"Philona!" he said and began scrambling down the sides of the cave. As he came the stars disappeared and the night sky paled and Thalamika thanked The Goddess they'd been in time.

Andrios jumped from a rock ledge to her side and took her in his arms and kissed her. Drupos spoke for the first time since they'd left the road. "By the Labrys! What *is* this? Last time I saw the two of you Thalamika was just learning to be properly civil to Andrios and now . . ." A gesture of comic bewilderment finished his sentence and made the others, even Philona who still showed the strain of the night, laugh.

"I'll explain later, Drupos," Thalamika said when they were sober again. "Now we've got to talk. Andrios should be away as soon as possible."

"Yes," Andrios agreed. "Come inside the cave in case a herdsman or charcoal burner should pass by."

They followed him and he stopped them within the entrance, just touched now by the growing light. He went on further into blackness and brought his thick wool cloak and spread it on the cave floor to protect them from the night damp.

"Now," he said, "tell me why Philona's here and how you managed to get her away from Phelleus."

"That had better wait, Andrios," Thalamika said. She wondered if they would ever have time to sit calmly and talk just about themselves like ordinary lovers. There was, certainly, no time now. "Phelleus was sending Philona away and Drupos heard of it and rescued her. We hope she knows more about the plots. There's been no time for questions before. Do you know anything, Philona?"

Philona took her hand from Drupos' and sat straighter on the cloak. "Yes," she said miserably, "and pray Zeus it's not too late."

She was shivering and her words came shakily. To give her a chance to steady herself, Andrios said, "Give us just the heart of it, Philona. No matter how you found out. You can tell us that later."

She said flatly, as if she were repeating a lesson learned by rote, "Yes. This is what I know. My father had plotted with the Mycenean Kretheus. Kretheus and his companions at the Court of Minos will, with the help of the Queen, seize the Palace and capture the Priest-King, killing him if they must. They mean no harm to the Young Prince. They intend to make him Priest-King in his father's stead, but he will have no real power. He will be a puppet of Lyssus. My father and the Mycenean merchants will cause a riot in Amnisos, so no help can go to Minos from the sailors of the war fleet now in port. My father has been chief among many Myceneans living in Crete who have set out to cause dissatisfaction among the farmers and artisans all over the island. The merchants hope and plan to provoke a general riot and profit by it to seize the power Minos now has over the shipping in the Great Green Sea. The lesser folk have been promised lower taxes and many other things when Minos is overthrown and Lyssus rules Crete in his place. The people in the countryside have been given arms brought in Mycenean ships and hidden in sea caves all around our island. When the trouble is well begun in Amnisos, my father will send a trusted slave to the top of Mount Juktas, where a signal fire is ready for lighting and a guard waiting for word to set the spark. When the first flame leaps on Juktas other fires on all the high mountains will be lit, calling the people to rise against their lords."

She finished the tale and added two bitter, hating words, "*My father!*" and hid her face against Drupos' shoulder.

No one spoke. They knew now what was planned for Crete and knowing it were held in silence. They had been afraid, but not enough. Such wide, careful planning! Such treachery, and such cruel lies! It was clear enough to all of them that, once the uprising had secured the kingdom for Lyssus, the men who had taken part would be destroyed in one way or another and the peasants and artisans would be no better than slaves. And this—all of it—was Kretheus' doing.

Andrios got up and went to the mouth of the cave and raised his clenched fists in the direction of Mycenae and shook them. "O Lord Poseidon," he prayed, "Ruler of the Sea, Earth-Shaker, Mighty Tamer of Bulls, put forth your hand upon Kretheus and Myrtis the Queen for their false dealing with your land and the people who have always delighted to honor you. Destroy them, Lord Poseidon, and save this land and this people, who hold you and the Earth Mother always in love and honor."

He stood there, looking down on the House of the Priestess, glowing like a jewel in the early light, until Thalamika said softly, "Come back, Andrios. There'll be time enough for anger and hating. Now we must think what to do. At least we know what to expect."

He came back as she bade him and sat close to her. "You're right," he said. "What we need now are clear heads and courageous hearts. Forget your shame for your father, Philona. You've done all you can to wipe that out. Now, tell me, are you *sure* of these facts you've given us?"

His words brought her a little comfort and she answered steadily, "Yes, Andrios. My father grew careless because he was going to send me away. Yesterday all the Mycenean merchants came to his work chamber beneath the room where he kept me prisoner. They didn't bother to keep their voices low and I heard them clearly. This was their last meeting, and each of them gave his report to my—to Phelleus. It was as I've told you."

"Was anything said of Mycenean warships?"

"No."

Andrios frowned. It seemed strange that there were no ships. He agreed with Minos that, without a war fleet, Lyssus couldn't hope to hold the island for long, no matter how much disaffection had grown among the peasants. Even if the Myceneans succeeded in disrupting the country for a while, the trained fighting sailors of Minos would soon bring order to the land. Still he wished he could be sure, wished he didn't have a nagging fear that somehow, somewhere there *was* a fleet. The Great Green Sea was full of islands, many of them uninhabited with wooded beaches, where a whole fleet of ships could be hidden. It would, he thought, be possible to send out many ships which looked as if they were meant for peace, then convert them in secrecy into a war fleet. Yet . . .

"Did you hear when they will strike, Philona?" Thalamika asked the question.

"I don't think they know the hour. That will depend upon Kretheus who, alone, will give the first signal. But it will be some time . . ." Her eyes opened wide. *"Andrios, so much has happened I'd forgotten what day this is. It will be some time today!"*

"Today!" Drupos had sat, quietly listening until now. "Today! Philona, why didn't you tell me at once, as soon as we met? Why didn't you . . ."

"Hush, Drupos," Thalamika said, seeing tears in Philona's eyes. "The Goddess knows Philona is doing all she can. You heard her. She lost track of time and so would you have done if you'd been in her place."

Drupos looked ashamed and took Philona's hand and kissed it and asked her forgiveness. "We're all tight with tension," Andrios said, dismissing the small incident. "Now let's not waste any more time. Today."

"But, Andrios," Drupos said, "today is the day of the Bull Games. No artisan or farmer would profane the Festival."

"No," Andrios agreed. "Nor any Mycenean merchant, for that matter, since Poseidon is the one god we have in common. Don't you see that this means we can count several hours before any action is taken? The Games and the Sacrifice will last all the afternoon. Then there'll be the feast and, if I know my own people, no one of them will stir until he's eaten his fill of the Priest-King's food, even if he does intend to do his best to destroy the provider later on. That will give us hours for thwarting the plotters."

"Thwart them!" Drupos shouted. Andrios warned him to be quiet, and he went on more softly. "How can we thwart them? We are only four—no, three because Philona must stay hidden—and they are many and their plans are well laid."

"Still," Andrios said calmly, "I think we *can* thwart them. In part at least. Enough." He grinned suddenly and they all felt better. "When haven't three Cretans been more than enough to thwart a hundred Myceneans? Besides we've got one big advantage over them. We know their plans and they don't know we know them. Now, Drupos, stop thinking up obstacles and listen to me. How long will it take you to get to the top of Mount Juktas?"

"Openly?"

"No. You must go in such a way you'll not be discovered."

"Three hours, then. Possibly four."

"Are you sure, Philona, there's no more than one man guarding the signal fire?"

"The one who spoke to my—to Phelleus of that part of the plot said they needed no more than one guardian for each fire."

"Then, Drupos, your job is to go to the top of Juktas, find the signal fire, knock out the guardian, and scatter the fuel pile so it can't be lighted. If that fire isn't lit, the others won't be and there'll be no general uprising. So we can forget the wider danger and deal only with trouble in Amnisos and Knossos."

Drupos grinned in his turn. This was a task to his liking. He'd see that signal fire was so scattered it would take a month to bring it together again. "I'll start now," he said and hesitated and looked at Philona. "But what about Philona?" he added. "I can't just go off like that and leave her. Where'll she go? What will she be doing?"

Andrios said, "Wait a minute, Drupos. We'll come to that. And, in any case, there's no sense in your rushing off until you've heard the rest of the plan. Philona, I think, will be safest right here. It's important her father doesn't find her or guess we know his plans. Will you be afraid to stay here alone, Philona?"

Philona's face went white but she shook her head firmly. The thought of cowering in the dark cave terrified her, but she'd not let them see it. Her family had done enough to cause trouble. She'd not add to it.

Andrios noticed her fear nevertheless, and he said, doing his best to reassure her, "I'll mask the entrance with brush so no one will know the cave is here. There's food enough and water, and we'll make a bed for you from our cloaks. Maybe you can sleep most of the day since you've had no rest all night."

He knew this wasn't much good. He hated to leave her alone, but he couldn't see anything else to do. He'd like to take her to his mother, but he didn't dare risk someone in Knossos seeing her. He frowned and looked at Thalamika uncertainly.

Thalamika said, "Why can't Chryses come and stay with Philona? She could watch while Philona sleeps and talk to her when she's awake. That way there'd be no need for Philona to feel forsaken and lonely."

Philona looked at once more cheerful, and Andrios and Drupos applauded Thalamika for her suggestion. Light was coming well into the cave now, and Andrios spoke again hurriedly. "Thalamika you must warn the Captain of the Nubian Guard. If you tell Nitos from me there's trouble, he'll not need Minos' agreement to put guards around the Mycenean embassy. He has enough authority to take precautions himself. Don't tell him more than you need and don't on any account mention the Queen. Nitos is half in love with her himself, I think, though what he sees in her is beyond me."

Thalamika nodded and he went on. "And another thing. I'm afraid you're going to have to watch Kretheus. I'm sure he won't hide himself today. If he's at the center of this thing, as he seems to be, he'll want to be seen as much and as openly as possible. Find him and stay close to him. Try to find out two things: if he's expecting support from the sea, and what time he plans to give the signal."

"Andrios," Drupos put in, "why do we need to know the time for the signal? Why don't we seize all the Myceneans now, at once?"

"Because we can't interfere with the Festival, Drupos. Besides if we act too soon, some of them may get away from us. It's likely enough they have some second plan if anything should go wrong before the signal is given, and not knowing what that second plan might be we don't dare risk letting them use it. I'm going to Amnisos and see the Captain of the War Fleet. . . ."

"No, Andrios! You mustn't. There's too much risk that . . ."

"Now, Thalamika," he said, touching her gently on the cheek. His voice was firm though his words were gentle enough, and she knew she'd better not speak so again. "There's risk in this for all of us, no more for me than for you and Drupos. Don't worry. I'll be careful. Now, can you deal with Nitos and Kretheus?"

"I'll deal with them," she said, wondering if she could be heard over her fear-sounding heart.

"Then look for me at the Games."

Again she wanted to cry out her dismay but she didn't, knowing it would bring her a rebuke.

"Now then. We'd better separate. You leave first, Thalamika."

He caught her about the shoulders and kissed her once and pushed her out of the cave entrance, where he stood and watched her until a turn in the path hid her from him.

CHAPTER
FIFTEEN

Thalamika kept her eyes steadily on the goat path down the mountainside until she came to the paved way beside the House of the Priestess. She wanted to stop where the path turned and look back and wave to Andrios, but she knew if she saw him again she'd lose her resolution and go running back and beg to stay with him. Her mind kept making pictures of Andrios, recognized, seized, and taken before the Priest-King for judgment. She forced herself to concentrate on the tasks he'd given her. Maybe if she thought of nothing else, she could forget her fear for him.

It was still early when she came to the House of the Priest-King. Workmen were busy in the Central Court, setting wooden barriers along all four sides to protect the Palace walls and pillars from charging bulls. Many people already stood on the walls. Some of them, she thought, had been there all night to be sure of a good place to see the Games. Minos and the Young Prince would be in the Inner Sanctuary, the most sacred of all the many shrines in the Palace, making ready with lustrations and anointings for the Festival. She thought of the Young Prince, proud and excited as he made his preparations for his first Festival. But most of the Palace people were still asleep.

She looked into the Guard Room. As she expected Nitos had not yet come to relieve the Captain for the Night, and she went on to her aunt's house. She'd have time to change her clothes and eat a proper breakfast. But first she must find Chryses and send her to Philona.

Chryses was waiting in the bedchamber, looking a little frightened because her mistress was not properly in bed. She wanted to attend to Thalamika's needs, but Thalamika insisted she leave immediately before the other slaves were about. They mustn't arouse any curiosity. Chryses left without further argument.

By the time Thalamika was freshly bathed and dressed and had eaten a meal, the whole of Knossos was awake and the sound of excitement seemed to burst from windows and doors. She went at once to the Guard Room, calling ahead for Nitos to come out to meet her. There was no answer and she looked inside. The Guard Room was empty. She was at first dismayed, then remembered what day it was and berated herself for a fool. Of course, the Nubian Guards would long since have been posted around the Palace, where they would be ready to control any pushing and shoving from the overeager crowd or break up fights that nearly always started at Festival time among artisans who'd celebrated with too much unwatered wine. She'd have to find him. He'd likely be outside the Inner Sanctuary and she'd have to go there. She shivered with awe. She didn't like even to pass this dread place, for it was associated with Poseidon in her mind and she could never feel anything but fear of the Bull Tamer.

Think of something else then. This was no time to be afraid.

Why was the House of the Priest-King so enormous? It would take time to reach the Inner Sanctuary, and then she'd have to tell her tale and pursuade Nitos to do as Andrios said. And that would take more time, for he was a stubborn and argumentative person, overproud of his position as Captain of the Guard. Even if he were a childhood friend of Andrios, she never quite trusted him. Never mind. Andrios had told her to find him and she'd have to get that over before she could carry out the second part of her task and search out Kretheus.

She hurried through the Hall of Many Pillars and up the stairs that led to the northwest portico and stopped short, holding her breath, as she came to a point where she could see up into the porch. Nitos was standing in the shadows of one of the red and blue columns across from the unfinished fresco of the charging bull. His saffron-colored kilts, edged with silver, and his sunburned torso and face were almost lost in the shadows. He had leaned the two spears which marked him Captain of the Guard against the column. The polished bronze spear heads reflected the sun, and it was their gleaming that had first caught Thalamika's eye. But what had stopped her was not the almost blinding light from the spears, but the other man who stood close beside Nitos, talking softly to him. The other man was Kretheus.

Neither of them had heard her, for they hadn't ceased their talk or looked toward the stairway. She turned away and went, carefully and quietly, back down to ground level, instinct rather than conscious reason warning her they'd better not know she'd seen them together.

She was at first only puzzled. She'd been too far away to hear any of their talk, but she'd thought, in the minute or two she watched, they had the look of conspirators. The full realization of what she'd seen struck her when she was halfway back down the stairs. And with realization came fear and near despair. Nitos and *Kretheus!* The Captain of the only armed force in Knossos and the leader of the revolt!

If Nitos and Kretheus had their heads together on this day in a place where they might properly think to find privacy, it meant, it *must* mean, that Kretheus had persuaded or bribed Nitos to take part in the uprising against the Priest-King. If she had found the Captain and told him what Andrios had said, Nitos would surely have given the message to Kretheus and that would have ruined all Andrios' plans. Surely The Goddess was protecting her today. She leaned limply against the side of the stairway and tried to think what to do now. Andrios would know, but she had no idea where he was. There was no way of warning him of this trouble, even if she had time, and there wasn't time. She must watch Kretheus. That, she thought, was even more important now.

Andrios had said he would be at the Bull Games. She'd have to talk to him then and trust to The Lady it wouldn't be too late. At least Drupos must be well on his way to destroy the signal fire, so everything would not be lost.

A sound from the stairs told her one of the men was coming down. The Goddess send it was Kretheus. She straightened and came around the side of the stairway and saw him midway upon it. She forced her face to a welcoming smile and waited where she was.

"Thalamika the Lovely," he called down to her.

"Where have you been? I've been searching the whole Palace for you."

Liar, she thought, and said aloud, "I've been about, here and there, watching the workmen." It would be safe enough to greet him with coolness. He'd think her angry because he'd deserted her. She made no move to go to meet him, and he took the remaining steps three at a bound and stood beside her.

"Don't be angry with me, Thalamika," he said, and she thought if she hadn't known his true thoughts, she'd have been entirely taken in by his gentle voice and seemingly sincere manner. "It hasn't been *my* wish to see so little of you these past weeks. There's been nothing for me but endless talks with Minos and his counselors, endless reviews of port duties and bills of lading and Zeus knows what else! But today, my lovely, I'm free. Your Priest-King has other duties and won't bid me come to his council hall for more of these fruitless discussions. And I've been looking for you so we might watch the bull leaping together. Will you come with me?"

He hoped he wasn't making a mistake, improvising in this way. He didn't like to act on instinct. He preferred to plan each detail of what he was going to do and plan it well in advance to test its worth. As he'd been doing these long weeks since he'd been an exile from his own loved land. This, he knew, was one reason why King Lyssus had chosen him to put into effect the great scheme to end the long and hated control of trade and the ships that went back and forth upon the Great Green Sea. He must not fail in the task his King had set him.

But what could he do? He'd come upon Thalamika too suddenly for planning. He'd forgotten her in these final

days of plotting, and when he'd seen her there at the foot
of the staircase he'd suddenly really wanted to be with her
at the Games. Zeus, she was beautiful! More beautiful
even than he'd remembered her as being. Something—
some little, fleeting thing—was different about her. He
studied her face but he couldn't put a name to the change
and went back to worrying about his sudden decision. He
couldn't see that any harm would be done. He'd planned
to be seen today—all day—by anyone who might have
wondered why he'd not been about the Palace lately. You
could fool a lovesick girl with tales of endless conferences
with Minos, but others would not be so easily misled.
Andrios, for instance. He'd an idea Andrios was suspicious
of him. He'd thought him a fool at first, but now he
wasn't so sure. What would Andrios think if he saw
Thalamika sitting with the Myceneans as the honored
guest of Kretheus? Surely her presence among them
would argue against Mycenean plots. She was a priestess
of their goddess. In spite of himself he shivered at thought
of the deity, for he'd been hearing tales of her anger and
her power and he could not entirely forget them. A
priestess would be above suspicion of treachery or con-
sorting with the enemy. On the whole, he thought his
last-minute decision was a good one.

He sighed. He'd been going to find Irata as companion
for the Games. Her clever and often cruel wit delighted
him. She knew all the gossip of the Palace and had no
scruples about telling it. Well, that was finished now. He
looked at Thalamika again and sensed again the difference
in her. She looked, he thought, somehow older and wiser;
certainly more desirable than he remembered her. But she
wasn't behaving more wisely. If she were a Mycenean

maiden, properly reared to know the lowly place of women and keep it instead of a bold Cretan thinking herself any man's equal, he'd woo her properly and win her too and take her home with him. In the meantime he might find her a pleasant companion at the Games. But what ailed her now? Why hadn't she answered his question?

"Thalamika?" he prompted her, touching her hair in the semblance of a caress which he almost felt.

She was startled by his gesture. She'd been watching his face as it changed with his changing thoughts, wondering what was in his mind. He'd stared at her, frowning, as if he were seeking in her face for the answer to some question and the stare had made her uncomfortable. Could he possibly have an inkling of what she was trying to do? That was impossible, she assured herself. But something was worrying him or puzzling him, and it had to do with her. She'd need to be very careful.

She called on all her knowledge of coquetry and forced herself to look at him as if she were, in truth, lovelorn. "You've deserted me for week, Kretheus." She pouted. "And I'm not sure your excuse is good enough. You couldn't have spent *all* your time with Minos."

"Be gracious, Thalamika," he wheedled. "I'm not my own man here in Knossos. If I were, I'd have spent every moment in your company. But here I'm only a representative of my King, and his business must come first with me. Do come with me to the Games."

"Well," She pulled her upper lip, pretending to be considering. "I *had* promised to go with Drupos. But if you *really* want me . . ." She let the sentence dangle, waiting to be urged.

"Of *course* I really want you. Say you've forgiven me

for staying away and understand the reasons. Say you'll be my lady for today."

"Oh—very well." She pretended to capitulate. "But you'll have to be very attentive to make up for your past conduct."

He seemed delighted, and she thought she'd fooled him well enough. So far so good. She'd managed neatly to stay with him, but The Goddess only knew how she could go about unlocking his brain to discover his plans.

From far down at the south end of the Central Court a dozen pipers blew a high, sweet call. Heralds stationed on all the walls cried out, "Take your places, ladies and gentlemen. Take your places for the Bull Games in honor of the Lady of the Labyrinth and Her Consort Poseidon."

Kretheus took her arm and said, "Come, then, my lady. One of my companions will give you his place in the front of the gallery which has been reserved for our use. I'll begin to make amends by seeing you have the best possible seat for the Games."

Thalamika thought, a few minutes later, he'd not been boasting. She did have the best possible seat, except for the place of the Priest-King. They were in the very front of a gallery close to the midpoint of the Central Court, seated upon bright-cushioned stools. They were the focal point of a crowd of chattering men and women, all of them in their gayest clothes. The expanse of the Court stretched before them. By leaning a little forward and looking up, she could see the long row of Horns of Consecration above the Sanctuary, where she was accustomed to offer the bloodless sacrifice. She could see, too, at the end of the Court, the two-stepped platform for the use of any leaper cornered by a charging bull. She wondered if any of the boys or girls from the Bull Court would use it today. A gang of workmen had just finished spreading a thick layer of sand over the smooth, polished stones of the Court and were leaving.

Minos and the Young Prince appeared at the top of the stairs leading from the Processional Corridor, and she leaned even further over the balcony to see them. Kretheus touched her hand and asked, "Are you pleased with your seat, Thalamika?"

"Certainly!" she answered, more sharply than she intended. She'd been listening, while she'd watched the final preparations, to his low-voiced conversation with a member of his embassy, and she was disappointed because their talk had been about nothing but the crowd and the coming Games. She was afraid she wouldn't learn anything from him and wished she could be sitting with Thalia and Amphidora and her other friends, even if their places were not ones of special honor.

He said, "What is it, my lady? Aren't you content?" He was, he realized to his own surprise, really concerned for her pleasure.

She must be more careful, she thought. She looked at him, hoping the look was languishing. "Of course, dear Kretheus. Who wouldn't be content to be sitting here with *you!* I'm the very envy of all my friends."

He had no time to consider his reaction to her flattery, for the pipers blew their shrill calls again and the crowd hushed and all heads turned to the south end of the Court. The Priest-King, in white kilts embroidered with gold and jewels, came down the stairway. Behind him, the Young Prince Sarpedon, already at twelve as tall as his father, looking proud and solemn at his first Bull Games, wore kilts of blue with a border of red stripes. On each wrist he wore a bracelet of porphyry and turquoise, and around his shoulders a chain of delicate gold lilies. His hair, long and unbound, was covered with a coronet of gold and turquoise, intricately fashioned in spirals and topped with three peacock feathers. He walked so lightly and with such grace he seemed almost to float, and again Thalamika was reminded of some winged creature whose proper element was the air. She felt a rush of affection for the boy who would now be counting himself a man, and she loathed Kretheus the more because he planned to make the proud young prince into a puppet of King Lyssus of Mycenae.

The next moment, affection and loathing were both forgotten, because, in the procession of the young men who followed Sarpedon and carried the vessels to be used in the sacrifice, she'd seen Andrios, resplendent in his finest kilts, holding the rhyton for the libation.

Andrios! The impulsive *idiot*. How could he be so careless of his own safety? If Minos knew . . . She looked quickly at the Priest-King crossing the Court toward the place kept for him. He seemed untroubled. His face showed no anger, only concentration upon his duties and, perhaps, pride in his son. Andrios must have slipped into his place after the procession had started. But he *would* be discovered and then what?

Kretheus touched her hand. She must pay attention. She fixed a smile on her face and turned to him.

"Tell me about the customs of this day, Thalamika," he said. She swallowed hard. She must forget Andrios, at least long enough to explain what Kretheus wanted to know. Remembering his past reactions to The Goddess, she thought she'd better not mention Her name. Poseidon was a god they had in common. She'd stick to him.

"Watch then, and I'll explain as the procession comes," she said. "These games are held in thanksgiving for the harvest, and Minos is today serving as High Priest of Poseidon. He and Sarpedon will go to their seats just there in the gallery above the Sanctuary of the Bloodless Sacrifice. The men in the procession are carrying everything that will be used later for the sacrifice. See the Labrys, the double-bladed ax? Minos will use it to kill the bull destined for Poseidon. He will wear that long, cloaklike robe over his kilts and the golden bull's mask when he pours the libation from the rhyton and mixes it with the blood of the sacrifice for the nourishing and strengthening of the God. See, the Labrys Bearer is setting it between the Horns of Consecration, where everybody can see it and where it will invite the presence of the God."

She wondered if she were babbling or sounded as if she were, but Kretheus nodded solemnly. Even these Cretans, he thought, paid proper honor to the Bull Tamer and these Games would, if they were what he'd been told, be a fitting tribute. "When will the Games begin?" he asked.

"Shortly now." She spoke absently, for she was watching Minos again. His throne had been placed just above the Sanctuary itself. He took his seat and looked over the Court. She saw his eyes jerk back to the place where the sacrificial vessels were being set up, saw him stare, and knew he'd recognized Andrios.

He turned his head to speak to Nitos, who, with three of the Nubian Guard, stood just behind the throne. Minos gestured and Nitos looked where he pointed and said something, and Minos shook his head. Thalamika thought he'd pointed out Andrios but forbidden Nitos to take action against him until the Games were done and the sacrifice made. Not even the Priest-King would dare profane the day until its end, and she thought she needn't worry for a while.

But how could she sit here and watch the leapers when all the energy of her mind and body was consumed in fear for Andrios? If she could only get him to look at her. She stared across the Court at him, willing him to find her among all the people and, as if The Goddess Herself were helping, Andrios placed the rhyton on the portable altar at the top of the Grand Staircase and turned to look over the crowd. The Lady must have directed his eyes, for he found Thalamika almost at once and raised an arm that seemed to take fire as the sun caught the jewel-studded gold bracelet above his elbow. She looked quickly at Kretheus. He was watching her closely, trying, she thought, to discover what held her interest in the Court. Would she endanger Andrios if she acknowledged his salute while Kretheus was watching her? She must take the chance. He must know she'd seen him. She turned sideways from Kretheus and raised her own arm in reply and saw Andrios make a slight beckoning gesture before he disappeared behind the barrier that protected the altar and all its sacred vessels.

Kretheus said, "Who is the fortunate one you salute, Thalamika? Your friend Andrios the Cupbearer, perhaps?" His voice held a peculiar note she couldn't identify, and she looked at his eyes but they were bland. She shook her head. "Andrios?" she repeated carelessly. "Did you see him? He's probably somewhere about the Court." She pretended to search among the votaries just finishing their tasks. "I haven't seen him. I was greeting my friends Amphidora and Thalia. See, they're just there, across from us."

She had no chance to gauge the effect of her words upon him. All about them the crowd was hushing again; people settling into their seats, stretching forward, waiting for the release of the first bull. She wouldn't worry any more. Andrios knew where she was. He'd indicated he wanted to see her when the leaping was done. He would find her or find a way to send her a message. She, too, settled upon her stool and prepared to enjoy the Bull Games.

CHAPTER
SIXTEEN

For the next two hours Thalamika, like the rest of the men and women of the House of the Priest-King sitting in the porches and galleries of the Palace, like the farmers and artisans, shepherds and woodcutters and charcoal burners who crowded the walls, forgot everything except the grace and skill of the teams of bull leapers. She felt pride in her land and her people grow almost to bursting as boys and girls not yet eighteen, two leapers and a catcher to each team, paraded around the Court. Beside her Kretheus complained that he couldn't tell one team from another since all were dressed alike in plain kilts and soft, white leather buskins and wore similar bracelets of precious amber on their wrists and above their elbows. She looked at him in genuine surprise. Anyone should be able to distinguish between the slight, taut bodies trained and honed to muscular skill and control, for each of the team members was individual in face and posture and style of movement.

"Where are their weapons?" Kretheus asked.

"Weapons?" she repeated. She must have misheard him, for surely there was no one in all the lands of the Great Green Sea who didn't know that the Cretan bull teams scorned weapons. "What weapons would they need except the skill of their minds and eyes and muscles? They don't want to *harm* the bulls, Kretheus, only outwit them and grapple them to the earth. Isn't it so in Mycenae?" She made the question sound artless, though she knew there were no bull teams such as these in his country.

He said defensively they didn't grapple bulls for sport in Argolis, only caught the wild creatures for sacrifice. He looked at her to see if she were intentionally trying to make him a fool, but she had turned again to watch the Court, empty now and ready for the first contest.

She had already forgotten Kretheus. She had seen four Bull Festivals at Phaistos and one other here in Knossos, since, at twelve, she had been allowed to attend her first Games. She thought, as the first team came running into the Court, she would never lose the heart-bursting excitement and delight of this day and nothing and nobody was going to spoil it for her.

Two girls, and a boy who held a knot of red linen, ran swiftly and gracefully as deer to a spot below the Priest-King and stood while he spoke the invocation to Poseidon, the Bull Tamer and to the Lady of the Labyrinth. When he was done, the team took its place at the north end of the Court and waited quietly until a door opposite was opened long enough to loose a bull.

The animal stood bewildered and frightened, pawing the sand, moving its huge, horned head from side to side. The crowd seemed not to breathe until the boy started to run, giving a high, shrill cry and waving his red knot. The two girls followed, pacing him, until they came to the midpoint of the Court. The bull, angered by the sound which was painful to its sensitive ears, bellowed defiance, raised its head, saw the boy, and charged.

Then there began a dance—graceful and teasing on the boy's part, awkward and angry on the part of the bull. Flaunting the knot up and down, sideways, tauntingly, maddeningly, the boy worked the bull into position. The bull made charge after charge at his tormentor who, running lightly, side-stepping, leaping away, never taking his eyes from the wicked horns seeking to catch him and toss him toward the sun, was always just out of reach.

When the bull was in line with the team's catcher, who waited, feet a little apart, arms outstretched, the boy tossed his knot aside and stood unmoving, waiting the next charge. The bull roared his challenge again and began to run. Head down; horns reaching; all four feet, it seemed, off the gound at once; the animal catapulted its huge body at the slight, still form before it. The boy didn't move until the horns, aimed at his stomach, were almost touching him. Then he sprang—straight at the bull. He caught a horn in each hand and using them for leverage vaulted over the bull's head, landed for a moment on his hands in the middle of the creature's back, twisted himself over and up and, just touching the catcher's hands for balance, landed with a little bounce on his toes beside the girl and ran lightly away to make room for the second leaper on his team, who was already beginning her somersault.

Team after team came and teased a bull and performed their leaps and left the Court. The spectators chattered and gossiped between demonstrations. But as soon as a new team appeared the thousands who watched were as silent as they would be later when the Priest-King sacrificed the chosen beast.

The last team performed as flawlessly as the first. No bull dancer had been hurt today. No bull had outwitted a single team.

Kretheus moved on his stool, relaxing muscles tensed with excitement. He looked at Thalamika and wondered why she was still sitting forward, still watching the empty Court. Was there more to come? "What will happen now, Thalamika?" he asked her, but she either didn't hear him or wouldn't heed him. He was irritated by her silence. No one treated Kretheus, Lord of Mycenae, with such discourtesy. He took her arm and shook it roughly and said, "Thalamika!"

"Hush," she whispered, "and watch," and he was suddenly aware that the spectators all over the Court were quieter than they'd been before.

At that moment the doors at the two ends of the Court opened simultaneously. Kastor, alone, looking small and helpless in the stretching spaces of the empty Court, came through one of the doors. From the other rushed the white bull captured in the defile.

Again, as in the demonstration, the man began to run toward the bull. But this time he was alone. And this time he must match his skill and wits against an animal not even partially tamed. This was to be the bull of sacrifice. If Kastor could not best it, he'd likely be gored, even killed, and another leaper would come and try to grapple the white bull to the ground.

Kastor gave no cry and flaunted no knot, for this bull needed no urging. No spectator moved. No sign from the watching crowd must be allowed to distract the attention

of the two creatures—human and beast—below. For uncounted minutes the bull dance went on. Twice it seemed
the bull would surely run its horns through the slight
body, and twice Kastor escaped seconds before the pointed
tips reached him. Sometimes the bull seemed to be chasing
the boy. At others it was plainly being led. And always the
boy conserved his strength as much as he could, while
the bull charged mindlessly, whirled and rushed and
charged again until it was plain that even its mighty body
was tiring.

Then came a time when the animal, breathing harshly,
stood in the center of the Court and rested, looking at
Kastor as if it would call a truce to this struggle. But
Kastor would give it no peace. He walked straight toward
it, keening now the tormenting cry.

The bull made a short charge. Kastor side-stepped. The
bull charged again, halfheartedly. Kastor moved again.
And again and again and again. And all the while Kastor
worked the bull toward the northwest corner of the Court,
toward the stepped stones that stood there.

At last the bull, a little rested now, seemed to decide
it had been tormented enough. It stood one more long
moment and Kastor let it stand, watching its eyes. Then
the creature began to run, straight toward the northwest.
Kastor, trained for months to minute timing, had gauged
the bull's intent and was already running before it. He
gained the stepped stone seconds ahead and leaped to the
top. The crowd gasped, knowing that Kastor had chosen
to execute one of the most difficult feats of the Bull Games.
The bull checked its rush, bellowed its anger and frustration, and put its front hoofs on the lower step, reaching
its horns toward the boy. They stood a moment so before

Kastor sprang from the step, seized the horns and, as the bull backed away, came with it, putting upon the horns the full pressure of powerful shoulder and arm muscles. The bull swung its head down, trying to loosen that hold. Kastor got his feet firmly on the sandy Court and braced them, arching his back, twisting his arms, giving the tired animal no chance to shake him loose.

A single moment the two seemed one. Then Kastor swung his body around, gave a final twist to his arms, and brought the bull's shoulders to the sand. The bull, off balance, lost its footing and fell, and before it could get up again Kastor had run, seemingly as fresh as at the beginning of the struggle, through the little gate in the barricade.

Even Kretheus was on his feet shouting and applauding the grace and beauty and precision of the feat, forgetting for the moment that he was a Mycenean, sworn enemy to this triumphant athlete and all his countrymen. When he went home again, he thought, he'd take the best of the bull teams with him and have them teach the Myceneans the sport. By Zeus, it was manly enough even for his war-bred countrymen.

All around him people were shifting in their seats, exclaiming over the fineness of the bull, the skill and strength of Kastor. There would, Kretheus gathered from their talk, be no more today, for this was the finest of all the bulls. It was a good omen, the Cretans were saying, that it had been brought low by the first grappler who had tried it. It was being taken away now, to be prepared for the sacrifice, and a fitting sacrifice it would make. Once the prize was awarded to the best demonstration team, everyone would go home and sleep for an hour or two until the westward-riding sun brought respite from the midday heat. That, Kretheus thought, was well. He'd welcome a rest after the excitement, and he'd need to be refreshed before the coming, new excitements of the night.

Thalamika watched the awarding of the prize without really seeing it. As soon as the white bull had been conquered, anxiety for Andrios had again rushed at her and filled all the corners of her mind. Was he safe? Was he well hidden? *Where* was he? She would have no more than two hours to find him and tell him of Nitos. And he might be anywhere in the vast Palace or the groves and gardens and parks surrounding it.

A mighty cheer that could be heard on Mount Juktas told her the prize had been awarded. She wrenched her mind away from Andrios. She'd have to deal with Kretheus before she could do anything else. Suppose he wanted to take her home! That would waste more of her short two hours.

Minos had risen from his throne and turned to leave. Would he send to search out Andrios now? She reassured her frightened heart. He'd go at once to the Inner Sanctuary to do whatever it was he did there. Nothing could be allowed to alter the ancient ritual of this festival day or displease the deities it honored. Andrios would be safe until the bull had been sacrificed. By that time she hoped he would be well away again from the Palace precincts. Why couldn't she keep that clearly in front of her mind?

Minos and Sarpedon left the porch, and the spectators began to leave their stools and their places on the walls. Kretheus said, "Shall I take you home, Thalamika, or . . ." and she interrupted, giving the first excuse she could think of for leaving him now, "No, Kretheus. I must first go to set out fruit and flowers before the Lady of the Labyrinth."

"Then I'll meet you here when we've rested," he said and was disturbed to know he looked forward to seeing her face again; troubled by the manner in which her beauty stirred him. Zeus, he must watch himself that he didn't become involved with this girl! At least not until Lyssus had all Crete at his mercy.

She agreed and went before him and managed to lose herself quickly in the slow-moving crowd. She looked over her shoulder once and saw him talking to Irata and breathed more freely, thinking he wouldn't check up on her story of setting out the bloodless sacrifice.

She managed, by wriggling and twisting and ignoring friends who called to her, to get clear of the crowd and into the long corridor that ran between the living quarters of the Palace and the storage rooms which held the pithoi of grain and oil. From there she went to the West Court. She thought Andrios might have hidden himself near the cypress grove and that would be the first place she'd look for him.

The West Court was crowded. Men and women were already propped in the shadow of its walls, dozing or eating or talking quietly in the noontime heat. Children, careless of the sun, played among the stalls, empty now and shuttered. A little girl ran toward her and took her hand.

"Thalamika," the child said, "do bend down. I have a secret."

The child, a member of her mother's family, was standing close to her, looking up at her with confidence that this older cousin would be interested in the secret. Thalamika was annoyed. She had no time now to play games with babies. She frowned and opened her mouth to speak sharply and send the small girl away, but before the words came she changed the frown for a smile. Who was she, she thought, to betray a youngster's trust? It would only take a minute. She knelt on the stone pavement and said, "Tell me quickly then, Helena. I'm on my way to sleep a while before the Sacrifice."

"Andrios told me to say he's in the room where the colors for the pictures are kept. He told me I mustn't tell anyone else. Only you, because you're his lady. Are you, Thalamika? Are you really his lady? That would be a nice thing. I *like* Andrios."

Thalamika hugged the child and whispered back to her, "Yes, Helena. I *am* his lady and I'm glad because I like him too. The Goddess bless you, small cousin. Now run home before your mother begins to fear you've been tossed by a bull!"

She kissed the dark curly head and saw the child run off in the direction of her home before she herself took a roundabout way that, though it appeared to go to her aunt's house, would as easily take her to the Quarters of the Fresco Painters. She should, she thought, have guessed Andrios would be there. He'd spent much of his boyhood in those shops, learning to spread the white plaster and mix clear, fresh colors for the pictures that gave warmth and beauty and interest to the rooms in the House of the Priest-King. She wondered, as she hurried to meet him, if Andrios would rather have been a fresco painter like his father than an administrator in the government of Minos. There were so many things they had still to find out about each other. Would there ever be time? Would they be alive at the end of this night?

She came cautiously toward the workshop area of the Palace, keeping careful watch for anybody who might report her presence and Andrios' to Minos. There was no one. The workshops, like the rest of the Palace, were quiet, drenched in the hot glare of the sun, resting. She passed through the antechamber, through a deserted room where half-finished sketches lay on tables and work-benches, into an inner storeroom for colors and brushes and the other tools of the artists.

It too seemed to be empty and she was again afraid. Had she been wrong? Had Minos' anger overcome his need to please Poseidon and The Lady? Had he sent to search for Andrios and found him and seized him?

A soft snore answered her inner questions and she looked toward the sound and found Andrios wrapped in his cloak in a dark, cool corner, quietly asleep. How could he, she marveled, sleep so in the face of his own danger? She wished she needn't wake him but she knew she must and went to him and leaned over and him and kissed him lightly on the forehead.

He was awake at once and alert, smiling up at her. "The small Helena found you quickly, my love," he said and got up in one smooth movement and took her in his arms and kissed her. But when she would have pro-longed the caress, he set her gently away from him, asking for her news.

She told him then of the meeting between Nitos and Kretheus and of her assurance that Kretheus had, by bribery or persuasion, gotten Nitos to join in his plot.

Andrios nodded, not speaking, looking stricken at this behavior on the part of his old friend.

"What can we do?" she asked, not able to bear the sorrow in his face.

"I think," he answered slowly, "Nitos must meet with an accident. The Nubians are well trained. They don't care who captains them, and they will, I hope, obey anyone who carries the two spears and the captain's sealstone. I wish I dared go to Minos again." She caught his arms, shaking them a little, and he smiled at her. "Don't worry, Thalamika. I'm not going. I know it would be useless. But we must have the Nubians with us. They must guard the Myceneans here in the Palace and see that none of them is free to seize Minos or Sarpedon. I've already seen the leader of the war galleys. He's an old friend of my father's and has always been suspicious of the Queen. He believed my tale and agreed to act without orders from the Priest-King. He's already armed those of his men who are in port and alerted them to keep the peace in Amnisos. But the Nubians *must* be subject to my orders."

He shook his head in a dazed sort of way. "I had thought everything was going so well and now this!"

She wanted to distract him. She said, "About Nitos . . ."

"I'll take care of Nitos after the Sacrifice." His voice was hard. "But I can't risk being seen again and I must know where he'll go when he leaves Minos." He was, she knew, thinking aloud and she said nothing when he stopped for a moment. "Can you find Spyros?" he asked finally.

"Spyros? Probably. He'll be with the other pipers near

the altar. But, Andrios, can you trust him? He's so—so frivolous!"

Andrios laughed a little. "You don't know Spyros, Thalamika. He uses frivolity as a cloak. There's no one in Knossos, except Drupos, I'd rather have beside me at need. Find him and tell him to follow Nitos and when he knows where he will go come to me here. Now, have you found out anything from Kretheus?"

She shook her head, feeling miserable and inadequate. Everybody, it seemed to her, was being helpful. Everybody except herself and all she was doing was failing Andrios. "I've listened, but he guards his tongue well. I don't dare ask questions for fear of making him suspicious."

"Never mind. You're doing all you can and finding out about Nitos is enough." His words comforted her. "Can you stay near Kretheus through the feasting, do you think?"

"Near enough. He'll certainly have to appear in the Great Hall. He won't want to be conspicuous and he certainly will be if he doesn't come to the feast. He may not ask for my company but he can't banish me from the Hall, and I'll manage to keep him in sight."

"Good. Watch him and try to come close enough to hear what he says." He thought a moment before he asked, "Do you think you could slip away unnoticed before the feasting's done?"

She nodded.

"Come straight to the old bastion where Spyros or I will be waiting and tell us anything you've been able to discover. Then, Thalamika, go *at once* to the cave. *At once.* There'll almost certainly be danger for you if you stay in the Palace area and I . . ." his voice shook a little, "I can't do what I must unless I know you're safe. Promise me this."

"Yes," she said, hating the promise, wondering why women must always wait in uncertainty while men acted. But she'd not hinder Andrios. "Yes, I promise. But, Andrios, be careful!"

As she took her seat once more beside Kretheus, Thalamika had to struggle to keep her breathing even. She'd found Spyros but only just as he came, at the last minute as usual, to take his place with the musicians. In a way she was glad of his near-tardiness, for he had no time to question her about Andrios' message and, in spite of Andrios' assurance of Spyros' stout heart, she didn't want to be the one to tell him what they feared. She'd had to run hard to get back to her place before the sacrificial procession began. Kretheus said, chiding her, "You were almost late, Thalamika. Were you keeping a tryst with some other man?"

She almost thought he was jealous! She answered shortly, "I was tired from the morning's excitement and overslept."

He looked at her sharply, and she was sure he guessed she was lying but he didn't charge her with it because the musicians had begun to play upon their pipes and lyres.

The sand had been cleared from the Central Court while it had been empty, and the loose stone above the pit for the blood sacrifice had been removed. The stones of the Court had been cleaned and polished and shone almost like jewels in the lowering sun. Pillars wreathed in flowers had been set up beside an altar near the open pit, and the double ax stood ready now between the Horns of Consecration in the center of the Court.

The musicians came slowly down the Court, followed by Priests and Priestesses of Poseidon in the skirts that simulated animal skins. A Priest led the white bull, quiet now, its horns garlanded with ropes of flowers. Just behind the bull the Young Prince carried a rhyton in the shape of a bull's head, black with gold horns.

Thalamika knew the figure following Sarpedon was the Priest-King. But knowledge was small armament against the sense of trembling awe that possessed her. Minos appeared in his long cloak to be taller even than Kretheus the Mycenean. His head was hidden by the gold bull mask so that he seemed less a man than some animal-god from the long-ago times of the stories.

He came to the altar and raised his hands in invocation to Poseidon. A Priestess filled the bull's head rhyton with wine from a clay jug and blessed the cup, and Sarpedon handed it to his father. Minos poured the libation and took the Labrys from the Horns of Consecration. The bull was brought forward and stretched upon a rack placed over the pit. Minos, with one deft thrust of the double-bladed ax, opened the beast's throat and the warm, red blood ran into the pit and mingled with the wine of the libation. The Priests and Priestesses raised a paean of thanksgiving to Poseidon, Lord of the Bulls and to the Earth Mother, and the Sacrifice was over.

CHAPTER
SEVENTEEN

Andrios waited in the shadows near the Court of the Bull Leapers. The last note of the paean had still been shivering in the air when Spyros had found him and told him Nitos would come this way, once he'd seen Minos and the Young Prince safely to the Inner Sanctuary. Spyros had been full of questions, and Andrios had told him quickly what he and Drupos and Thalamika knew of the night's plots. Spyros had wasted no more time in questions. He'd only asked, "Can I help?" and his voice had been tight with anger, and laughter had gone from his eyes.

"Yes," Andrios said. "Come with me to the edge of the Bull Leaper's Court and whistle when you see Nitos. When we're sure he'll give no trouble, we'll think about our next move."

They had gone then at once to their stations. Spyros had stopped in a grove of pines not far from the Court and watched Andrios until he was lost in the long purple shadows of the dying afternoon.

As he waited Andrios wished Nitos would hurry. Minutes seemed to have taken wings, and each one that flew away meant so much less time to do what must be done.

He eased his position cautiously, trying to lessen the tension growing in his mind.

Would Minos already have sent to search him out? How long would it be before he was discovered? Had Nitos changed his mind and taken another way to his quarters? What if . . . ?

Spyros' low whistle gave the warning and put an end to the waiting. Andrios flattened himself sideways against the wall and squinted around its angle. The Captain of the Nubians was crossing the grassy plot before the Court, coming quickly, carelessly, his two spears held loosely over his shoulder, humming to himself. He was very close. Andrios eased away from the wall and stood as he had so often done when he was waiting for the rush of a bull, feet close together, arms outstretched. Now he could hear Nitos breathing; but he waited until the Captain was well past his corner before he lifted his body in a leap and launched himself forward.

The spears flew from Nitos' hands and he hit the ground with a thud that knocked him windless. Before he had time to regain breath, Andrios had covered his mouth and called softly to Spyros, who came running.

"Take the cloth from my belt and stuff it into his mouth, Spyros, while I hold him. Then we can tie him up and hide him until the night's affairs are done."

Nitos struggled and made meaningless sounds behind Andrios' hand, but Andrios was the stronger and held him until Spyros had him tied. Andrios tested the knots on his prisoner's hands and feet and made sure the gag couldn't be worked out. When he was satisfied, he said, "Where shall we hide him, Spyros?" and Spyros pointed to one of the stone-circled pits used to store grain. "That one's empty," he said. "I saw them taking the last of the old grain out of it yesterday. He'll be safe enough there."

Nitos thrashed about on the ground and tried to speak, but the others paid him no attention.

"You take his feet, Spyros. I'll take his shoulders—as soon as I have *this*." Andrios stooped over the bound man and took off the sealstone that swung on a gold chain about his neck. "I wish I could have a token from Minos himself, but this will have to do. The Nubians will recognize and I hope honor it, no matter who wears it." He took off his own seal and put it carefully inside his wide belt and placed the seal of Nitos around his own neck. "Now," he said, stooping to get his hands under the Captain's shoulders.

Nitos arched his back, making his body as heavy as possible, digging his bound feet into the ground.

Andrios cuffed him roughly in the face. "Be still, traitor," he said, "and thank Poseidon this is his Festival day. Killing is what you deserve for betraying your trust, but you'll live, for Poseidon's sake and for the sake of our old friendship. Not even your treachery can entirely erase its memory. You'll be safe enough in the grain pit and tomorrow Spyros will come and free you. But then you'd better go to your friends in Mycenae as fast as a ship can take you, for if I find you here I *will* kill you. Ready, Spyros?"

They picked him up and took him to the pit and lowered him, roughly enough, but careful that his head wasn't broken by the stones at the bottom. "Stay there," Andrios said, "and consider where treachery leads."

"What now?" Spyros asked, dusting his hands against his kilts.

Andrios stooped to get the two spears before he answered. "It will be dark soon, and I'll need darkness if I'm not to be discovered, darkness and the beginning of the feast. I don't think trouble will start until the feasting is over. Kretheus—may the Earth-Shaker blast him—will know it will be easier to take even the peace-loving Cretans if they are full of food and wine and ready for sleep. We'd as well go back to the Quarters of the Fresco Painters and wait there."

"Won't there be danger for you if one of the painters should find you?"

Andrios laughed. "Not from the fresco painters. I've known them all since my father took me among them before I could walk. They'd hide me from The Goddess Herself."

Spyros said, "I think your plan's good, then. But it might be as well if I go to my own house and bring food, for I doubt we'll eat the Priest-King's food tonight."

"Yes," Andrios said, "but be cautious. Be sure you're not seen coming or going."

"Don't worry. No one will see me," Spyros said, and Andrios believed him, for the next moment he'd vanished and Andrios hadn't seen him go.

Andrios went at once to the Fresco Painters' Workshops. The anteroom was dark but a lamp had been lit in the workroom beyond and spilled enough light through the door to show the way. He wondered who was inside and drew in his breath when he saw his father stooping over one of the benches examining a sketch drawing. Andrios wondered how much his father knew of the quarrel with Minos and its results. Maybe it would be best if his father didn't see him and so could say honestly, if asked, he knew nothing.

Andrios turned toward the outer door again. His father, without looking up, said, "Andrios. Don't go away."

Andrios said, "Father, it's better if you don't know where I am. I—I'm under sentence of banishment. Minos . . ." His voice broke in spite of his efforts to keep it calm.

"Yes," his father said. He sounded heavy and tired. "I know all that, my son." He turned then and looked at Andrios, who had come into the room and stood beside him. "Something—something strange is happening in Crete and I don't know what it is. There's a feeling . . ." He stopped himself and took a deep breath and went on. "I know, Andrios, there's no time now for explanations. I'm wondering—wondering whether I should give you the message I've brought here for you."

"What message, Father?" Andrios felt his scalp prickle. He'd never seen his father like this, uncertain, almost dazed, and it frightened him. His father didn't answer, and Andrios said, "you'd better tell me, Father. Then, between us, we can decide what to do."

His father lifted his shoulders and dropped them. "I'm afraid, Andrios. Afraid of a trap which, knowing you well, you'll walk into, thinking it your duty to do so."

"Tell me," Andrios said and gripped his father's shoulders until the older man winced. "I give you my promise I'll not do anything foolish."

"A while ago," his father said slowly, "young Sarpedon came to my house looking for you. He was white and frightened. He asked if I knew where you were and I said no, though I thought you'd probably come here if you wanted to hide. He looked at me—I'd swear it was genuine—with despair. He said that after the Sacrifice he'd left his father in the Inner Sanctuary and gone to put aside his Festival clothes and bathe and dress again for the feasting. Minos stayed behind, saying he wanted to offer private sacrifice to The Goddess, for he was troubled and fearful for his people. He told the Young Prince to come to him there later, and when the boy returned he found the Priest-King fallen before the altar and moaning in pain. Sarpedon tried to help him and could do nothing and would have called the Guard. But Minos stopped him and told him to find you and bring you to him."

"Minos, Goddess-stricken!" Andrios forgot everything except love and pity for his uncle. "I'll go quickly."

"Andrios! This may be a ruse to get you in his power."

"No, Father," Andrios said. "Don't you see? Minos wouldn't have sent the boy upon such an errand. Will you stay here until Spyros comes and tell him to wait for me—or for word from me?"

"Andrios!" his father cried out, as if he too were in pain. "Be careful," but Andrios didn't hear, for he was already running toward the Inner Sanctuary.

The guardian Nubians crossed their spears threateningly before the door of the shrine. Andrios threw over his shoulder the two spears he'd taken from Nitos and showed the Captain's sealstone. They looked at him curiously, but they saluted and let him through and he breathed more freely, knowing that his guess about their obedience to the symbols of office had been good. At least so far. He had no time to think further now. He crossed the outer room in two long paces and thrust open the door

—upon darkness. He stood listening, stretching his mind into the quiet room, but he could hear no sound.

He said, "Sarpedon?" and was answered by a sob and almost reeled backward as the Young Prince threw himself upon his friend. Andrios put both arms around the boy and held him tight for a minute before he said, knowing action would steady the boy more than sympathy, "Get a lamp, Sarpedon, and send one of the Nubians for the High Priestess."

The shrine seemed still and empty, and Andrios wondered if Minos were already dead, then heard with relief the sound of breath drawn in a slow and painful gasp. Sarpedon came back with a lighted lamp and held it high so Andrios could see the straight-backed stone throne and behind it the wall decorated with frescoes of the sacred lilies. He could see, too, the fallen bulk of the Priest-King beside a circular stone altar covered with fruit and flowers ready for sacrifice to The Goddess.

Andrios knelt beside Minos and put his arm under his uncle's head, and held it up to ease the rough breathing. The Priest-King still wore the ceremonial cloak. It had crumpled under him when he fell, and Andrios wished he could raise the fallen man enough to get it out but didn't dare. The Priest-King's right hand was clenched about the gold bull mask. His eyes were closed, his face was mottled red and white and his mouth was twisted with pain.

The light wavered and Andrios looked up and saw Sarpedon shaking so he could hardly hold the lamp. "Put it in the wall niche, Sarpedon," Andrios said gently, "and come here beside me."

He turned back to Minos and said, "It is I, Andrios,

my uncle. I've sent for the High Priestess. She'll bring healing herbs to help you."

Minos opened his eyes and looked at Andrios and said, in a wracked whisper, "No—time. I'm—dying—Andrios." The whisper stopped and Andrios waited, hearing the Young Prince sob beside him, wanting to sob himself. Minos took another slow, agonized breath and went on. "You—were—right—about—the Queen." Andrios would have hushed him, but he seemed to gather what little strength he had and went on more strongly. "She came to me here and taunted me and said the Myceneans would have my whole country by morning. They've poisoned my own people against me. Even—even Nitos. And—a signal—"

Andrios said, "I know, my uncle. I know about Nitos and the signal. Don't worry. Nitos is bound and hidden, and I have his seal and spears. Drupos the Boxer has gone to destroy the signal fire. Sailors from your war fleet are guarding all the houses of the Mycenean merchants in Amnisos. The kingdom is safe or will be when we've secured the Mycenean embassy. Rest now until the High Priestess comes."

The Priest-King's eyes lost some of their haunted look, but he still struggled with his troubled breathing, trying to speak. Andrios leaned closer to him. "Mycenean—fleet—coming. Warn our crews. War—fleet—must be—ready."

Andrios' heart jerked. This was what he'd feared, and he wondered what they could do and knew he mustn't think of that now, for Minos was speaking again.

" . . . my—son to your care. I—want—to—see him—anointed—and—invested—before I die. Sarpedon!"

Andrios could feel the shaking of the Young Prince's body against his, but Sarpedon controlled his sobs and put his hand on his father's hand and said, steadily, "I'm here, Father."

Once more Minos seemed to gather strength to speak to his son. "You're overyoung to be Priest-King, my son. But the ways of The Goddess are just, and you must very soon take up my burdens. Trust Andrios. Be guided by him until, when you are four years older, he takes you to the cave of our Cretan Zeus to receive the laws as I received them and all your ancestors. Rule justly. Honor The Goddess and Poseidon. Grow in wisdom and courage."

"I—I'll try, Father. But—but . . ."

Andrios put his free hand on Sarpedon's shoulder and gripped it hard. Minos closed his eyes again, but the slow, heavy breaths still came. The lamp sent a flickering light over the shrine—over the flower-decked altar and the alabaster jar that held the sacred oil and over the still, clear water in the oblong lustral basin sunk in the middle of the room. Would the Priestess never come?

The thought was hardly complete when he heard the light swish of her bare feet on the stone floor and saw her in the doorway.

She came quickly to Minos, her old, wise eyes tear-filled. She, too, knelt beside him and put her ear against his chest and laid her hand gently on his forehead, wet with the sweat of his pain. "It's come, then, old friend," she said, and he opened his eyes and tried to smile and said, "Yes."

Andrios whispered furiously, "Help him!" and she

looked at him and shook her head and said, "I cannot. There's no healing herb to mend a worn-out heart."

Minos said, "Quickly. The—sacred—oil," and she went to the stone bench to get the jar. "Take—my—seal—Andrios." Andrios took the heavy ring that had so recently cut his cheek, surprised at how easily it came off the Priest-King's thin finger. "Give—it—to—Sarpedon." Andrios handed the seal ring to the Young Prince, who held it as if it had been a scorpion. "This is the sign of your kingship, my son. Use it wisely."

The Young Prince made a sound they took for a promise. He couldn't form the words.

The Priestess came back with the jar of oil. Andrios led the Young Prince to the lustral basin and bathed his feet and hands and poured water over his head in the ceremonial cleansing from evil. The Priestess anointed him with the sacred oil, sweet with perfumes of many flowers, and said, "This is the sign of your Priesthood, Sarpedon. Go now to your father and receive his blessing."

The Young Prince, as if he had been physically changed and strengthened by the water and oil, walked steadily to Minos and spoke clearly, unwaveringly, the words he'd been taught as soon as he could speak plainly, "Will you my King, High-Priest of the Earth Mother and Her Consort Poseidon, give me your blessing and endow me with the power of the Bull Tamer?"

Minos tried to lift the bull mask but he hadn't the strength. He whispered, "Take it, Sarpedon, Prince of Crete, Priest now and King of the land of Crete. Honor always The Goddess and Poseidon."

The Young Prince leaned down and took the mask and held it uncertainly, not sure what he should do because, by the ritual that had existed since man's memory could tell of it, the mask should be placed on the new King's head by a Priest. Sarpedon looked at Andrios, and Andrios signed to him and he lifted his arms and put on the mask.

The Priestess came to the boy and bowed before him and touched the mask and the seal and stepped back for Andrios to do the same. She raised her arms then and spoke in a high, light voice, unlike her own, "Bear witness, O Gracious Lady of the Labyrinth, Great Goddess, Earth Mother; and you, O Poseidon, Earth-Shaker, Lord of the Bulls, bear witness that Sarpedon, Son of Minos, is named Priest-King to rule over the land and the people of Crete and all the possessions of the land, when the soul of Minos shall leave his body to live forever in the blessed land of the dead."

As she finished, the room seemed to take on an added brightness. Andrios lifted the bull mask from Sarpedon's head and laid it beside the Priest-King again. Sarpedon dropped down beside his father, a boy once more, heart-riven. Minos took his son's hand and, as if the touch restored his health, sat straight up. His eyes were fixed upon a spot just above the altar stone and he spoke in the voice of a young man, full of strength and beauty. "Hear me," the young voice said, "while I prophesy. Not yet will the peace-loving people of Crete be ground beneath the heel of the war-god of Mycenae. Poseidon, Earth-Shaker, will send destruction upon Kretheus, Prince of Mycenae, who would have profaned The Goddess, and upon Myrtis of Mycenae and upon their plans. Blessed be the name of the Earth Mother and Her Consort Poseidon."

He drew one more breath. Then his muscles that had been taut relaxed slowly, and he fell back upon the floor.

CHAPTER
EIGHTEEN

The Priestess looked at the face of the Priest-King, quiet now and pain-free, and shook her head at Andrios. But Andrios didn't need her sign. He had known at once that Minos was dead. He stood, looking down upon the man he'd loved as kinsman and honored as Priest and served as King, wishing he could take time to grieve a while with his young cousin, knowing he must lay aside sorrow until the country was safe.

Tomorrow, if they were still free, if they could win freedom against the Mycenean war fleet no doubt already nearby and waiting only a sign from Kretheus, Minos would be taken with honor to the royal tomb and laid beside his father and his brother. Tomorrow the Young Prince would sit upon the throne in the Hall of Justice and hear the pleas and complaints of his people and, with his counselors, judge between them according to the ancient and god-given laws. But tonight Sarpedon must be taken quickly to a safe place. If necessary, if the Myceneans should succeed in spite of all their efforts, Andrios thought he would take Sarpedon—and Drupos and Thalamika and Spyros and Philona—by stealth to the other side of the island and from there to the

Land of the Pharaohs until they could find a way to re-
store the new King to his throne. But first he must get
Sarpedon away. Then he could attend to other things. He
wished he could seek out the statesmen who had aided
Minos in running the kingdom. They would not have
listened to him when he was under banishment. Now
they were among the feasters, and there was no time to
seek their advice and aid.

He looked across the body of Minos to the Priestess. She stood straight and quiet, remote from human
grief as she was from human joy, Goddess-possessed,
and relief filled his mind. He could as safely leave Minos
with her as with The Goddess herself, for The Priestess
was held in only a little less awe. Not even Myrtis, the
Queen, would dare disobey her orders when she was at
one with The Lady.

"I must go, O Priestess," he said, "and take the Young
King with me. There's danger for him and for the land."

She nodded, not losing her rapt look. "I know of it,"
she said in a voice unlike her own and he wondered
how, and she seemed to comprehend his wonder, for she
went on, "as a Priestess of the Earth Mother knows many
things, yet may not reveal them. Take the Young King
quickly to the hills and hide him until the time comes, for
many dangers will walk in Knossos tonight and he must be
away. I, alone, will keep watch beside Minos and prepare
his body for burial, and none must know of his death
until Crete is safe again."

"The Queen," Andrios said, "the Queen knows. She
came here and taunted him."

"Myrtis knows nothing. She left this place before

Minos fell nor stayed to see him heart-riven by her treachery. Now go, for there's little time."

Andrios shivered at the sound and look of her. He
thought, for the first time since he'd come pell-mell to find
Minos, that he shouldn't be in this place, where only those
dedicated to The Goddess came. He wondered if The
Lady would smite him for sacrilege and knew on the instant she wouldn't, because Her Priestess had accepted
his presence as necessary. He put his hand on the boy's
head and said, "Sarpedon."

The boy, who was again kneeling beside his father,
didn't move or look up, and Andrios said again sharply,
"Sarpedon! Leave your grieving. Minos has gone to live
with the shades, and tears won't bring him back."

Sarpedon did look up then, and Andrios saw there were
no tears in his eyes though the marks of weeping were
still on his face. His eyes held something of the same
look as the Priestess' eyes. He got up and stood very
straight and Andrios thought he'd grown taller in the last
hour. "The land is troubled, Andrios," he said, "and
I must lead my people."

"Not tonight, Sarpedon. Tonight I'm going to send you
to the hills with Spyros the Boxer, the Ever-laughing."

"NO!" Sarpedon said.

"Obey Andrios the Cupbearer, O Sarpedon, Priest-King
of Crete. That is the will of the Earth Mother and Poseidon. Your time for leading your people is not yet come."
The Priestess didn't look at the two opposite her, but her
voice rang on the order and Sarpedon was quiet.

Andrios said, "Do you grant me right and leave to act
for you tonight, Sarpedon?"

"Yes, Andrios the Cupbearer."

"Then give me the seal of Minos that is now your seal, so my orders won't be questioned."

Sarpedon handed him the seal he'd been holding tightly since Minos had given it to him. Andrios put it on his finger, feeling it a little loose but not too much for safety. The Priestess picked up the bull mask and held it out to the new Priest-King. She didn't speak, but she seemed nevertheless to have communicated something to the boy, for he smiled bleakly at her and nodded and fastened the mask to his belt. Andrios felt the hair stir on his neck at this understanding that needed no words. They were now, both of them, Goddess-dedicated he thought, and he himself felt small and alien and awe-filled in their presence. Yet it was he who must act.

He said, "Come," and Sarpedon, straight and proud, walked before him out of the room.

Andrios stopped him when they came to the outer door where the Nubians stood, silent, unmoving. Andrios showed them the spears and the Captain's seal and ordered the men to follow him. One of them, a sergeant, shook his head, refusing to leave his post even if, for some reason he couldn't understand, they had a new Captain who issued strange orders. "The King," the sergeant said and pointed within.

"The King," Andrios said quietly, "is guarded by the High Priestess. No harm will come to him." He held out the Priest-King's sealstone and, at sight of it, the sergeant made an obeisance. "The King bids you do as I say. Follow."

The sergeant spoke to his fellow guards in the Nubian language and they raised their spears, saluting Andrios and his companion, and came after them, keeping an exact two paces behind.

Andrios led them quickly to the Quarters of the Fresco Painters and into the workroom where he had left his father. The older man's head was bent, and Andrios thought he was weeping. Andrios touched his shoulder and he turned and gave a small cry of joy and relief and put his hands on his son's arms. Andrios said quickly, "The banishment is lifted, my father, but I've no time to explain now. Tomorrow I'll tell you all that has happened. Is Spyros here?"

"Here, Andrios." Spyros had a mouthful of honey cake, and his words came muffled. At another time Andrios would have laughed as his friend almost choked in his haste to swallow, but he had no laughter now. "Do you know the cave above the House of the Priestess, Spyros?"

"Yes," Spyros said, coming into the circle of light thrown by the lamp. He saw Sarpedon and the two Nubians and his eyes opened wide and he said, "What . . . ?"

Andrios cut him off. "No questions, Spyros. Take the Young Prince to the cave. At once. You'll find others already there. Wait with them for me. Go with them," he added to the Nubians, "and guard them well. If anything happens to them, you'll never see your homes again."

He didn't wait for an answer. He touched his father's hand lovingly, gripped Sarpedon's arm, and left the room, running.

A full moon lit the Central Court of the House of the Priest-King, empty now except where the Nubians stood guard. As Andrios ran toward it he was conscious that he was very tired and hungry. His head felt light and his mind refused to focus on what he must do. He'd have to find food. This was no time to collapse from hunger, and he'd eaten nothing since last night. He veered from his course and crossed the Hall of the Double Axes and the Queen's Hall, empty and dim, to the corridor that led to the kitchens. They, too, were empty, for all the kitchen servants had taken their portable braziers to the Great Hall to serve the feast. A fowl, forgotten, had been left behind on a table, and Andrios took it and stood, gnawing at it hurriedly, washing it down with a cup of coarse wine from a pithoi in the corner.

The food helped clear his head, and as he ran on again he began to plan. They couldn't wait now for sure knowledge of the time the revolt would start. He'd re-post the Nubians, instruct them to seize Kretheus and the rest of the Myceneans just as soon as the feasting was over. He must get to Amnisos and warn the Captain of the War Fleet to expect Mycenean ships. Or could he leave that? He should also be on the bastion when Thalamika came, now that Spyros had taken the Young Prince to the cave. But did he dare believe the Mycenean fleet would wait to attack the port and the ships in it until the signal beacon had been lighted on Juktas? No, he didn't dare. He'd have to go to Amnisos. He must see with his own eyes that the Mycenean merchants were secured by the Guardians of the Peace, see what sailors could be spared from the warships to reinforce the Guardians. He'd have to trust that Thalamika, finding no one at the bastion, would go at once to the cave as she'd promised. He ran toward the first guard post, putting everything from his mind except what he must do.

Thalamika stood in the Great Hall watching Kretheus and the Queen. She had, she thought, been there for hours upon hours. The Hall was blazing with light from a hundred lamps standing against the walls or set in niches in them. Dozens of men and women, resplendent in their best clothes, milled about the huge room between tables decorated with fruit and flowers that took the light and reflected it in glowing colors. The room was noisy with shrill talk. The guests kept turning their heads to watch the door, expecting the coming of the Priest-King. They were curious to know what kept him and irritated, for they were hungry and the smells of roasted meat and spices and new-made bread were tantalizing.

Thalamika edged closer to Kretheus and the Queen. She *had* to hear what they were saying. Andrios was counting on her. She hadn't been able to get near Kretheus when he had come into the hall because of the crush of older statesmen and their wives, all anxious to greet the Mycenean. He wore a red tunic edged with gold and his short curls were bound with a gold fillet. His eyes had been excited and glittering, and she thought again of the fabled basilisk. He was smiling and there was something hectic in his gaiety.

The Queen had obviously been waiting for him. She, too, seemed overexcited. She stood apart from her guests, scowling as usual, flanked by her two Mycenean serving women, who seemed to be acting as guardians against anyone who tried to come near their mistress. Myrtis was dressed tonight in a long, loose gown of gold cloth, belted with jewels, her arms and shoulders bare as if she would flaunt her Mycenean birth before the flounced and corseted Cretan ladies. The folds of her gown went in and out as the Queen tapped the floor in impatience. But impatience did her no good. Kretheus made slow headway. Again and again he was stopped by guests and he could not, without calling unwanted attention to himself, pull away from them.

It was easy to keep him in sight in spite of the crowded room. His blond head showed well above the small, dark Cretans, and Thalamika followed it until it came at last to the Queen. Thalamika moved nearer by inches, keeping knots of guests between herself and her quarry, fretting that she didn't dare go boldly and quickly.

Still Minos didn't come. Thalamika listened to the noise in the room and judged the growing tension by its mounting volume and shrillness. Where was Minos? Why didn't the Queen send to get him? A larger group of guests came between her and Kretheus, and she was able to move quickly a full two feet nearer.

Had the plotters murdered Minos, or already secured him? No, she answered her own question. The Queen and Kretheus looked as puzzled as the rest, turned as often to the door. Kretheus was frowning. She moved a little closer. The Queen's voice rose briefly and Thalamika heard a few words, ". . . in the Inner Sanctuary when I left him . . ." before Kretheus shook his head and the Queen dropped her voice again to a murmur.

What had the Queen been doing in the Inner Sanctuary? No one was supposed to enter that sacred and secret shrine except the specially Goddess-dedicated. Even Thalamika, Priestess though she was, had never been allowed there.

She must get closer, hear more.

In her anxiety she forgot caution and moved boldly,

and at the same time another shifting of the restless guests
took away her screen and she found herself looking
directly into Kretheus' eyes. The Queen saw her, too,
and pointed and said sharply and clearly to Kretheus, "The
girl Thalamika. She spies. One of my women . . ." She
stopped, realizing that Kretheus wasn't listening.

He hadn't seen Thalamika since he'd come into the
Hall, and he'd been wondering where she was. He
couldn't take his eyes away from her. She had chosen to
wear tonight a dress of deep, brilliant blue, threaded with
silver and cut low over a filmy chemisette of white. Her
arms were bare almost to the shoulders and the narcis-
sus white of her skin was set off by jade and turquoise
bracelets exquisitely chased. Her eyes and lips were just
touched with color, and her black hair gleamed without
the need of unguents. All his senses stirred at her
beauty, and he made an involuntary movement toward
her.

The Queen said, urgently, softly, "Kretheus! She's dangerous. Get her away!"

The words meant nothing to him. What was his
cousin saying? *Who* was dangerous? Not the little, the
beautiful Thalamika. No one with such beauty could be
dangerous.

"Kretheus!" The Queen spoke his name so sharply the
word came to him as the sound of a javelin piercing a
bull's hide shield. Thalamika heard it too, and knew she'd
overplayed her spying game and started to retreat toward
the door of the room.

Kretheus wanting to be beside her called, "Thalamika,
don't go. Wait for me," and started after her. She began

to run, elbowing and pushing her way, not caring what she did so long as she got away from him.

The Queen said, "Go after her, Kretheus. She knows something," and the words and Thalamika's guilty hurry shattered his bemusement, and he was suddenly afraid for all his plans and deeply ashamed that he had allowed himself to be bewitched by this deceiving girl. Myrtis was right. Thalamika *was* dangerous. He knew now, intuitively, what in her was changed. She was no longer a wayward child. She had grown in these last weeks into womanhood and she was clever. He felt cold. He shouldn't have spent this day with her. What had he said? Had he given away anything of his plots? He couldn't have. He told himself he wouldn't have been that besotted by even her great beauty. But he couldn't be sure, and the fear that he had failed his King and his mission was a sickness in him. Had he betrayed his trust for a beautiful face? Maybe it wasn't too late. If this clinging crowd would only open and let him through, let him get to her before she could find Andrios, he'd kill her. But the crowd continued to cling, and she was getting away from him. He must hurry.

Thalamika reached the door well ahead of him, but she knew her slight start would mean little once he was clear of the room. His longer legs and greater strength would soon overcome her lead. She had only one weapon against him. She knew the twistings and turnings of the Palace, the corridors and stairways and innumerable rooms opening one into another, better than he.

In her haste to be away from what she knew was real danger (for she was sure he wouldn't hesitate to hurt her, even kill her if it suited him), she hadn't thought where she was going. Now she must decide and quickly. Andrios or Spyros should be on the bastion waiting for her, but the way to it was direct and she would never make it in safety. If she could dodge among the porches and in and out of the rooms that bordered them, if she could get as far as the south end of the Central Court, she could go down a small inner staircase she knew of. It led right through the outer wall and she could lose herself in the night.

She ran down the beautiful marble stairs from the reception halls on the second story of the Palace to the Court, not feeling the cool stone on her bare feet. She couldn't take time to get her shoes. She had already turned the corner before her mind registered the fact that the Nubian Guards were absent from their proper places at the doorway. She prayed The Goddess as she ran that Andrios had rid them all of Nitos.

She was halfway down the length of the Court when she heard Kretheus behind her and turned her head and saw him running. A stone lamp, unlit, stood against a pillar and she ducked around it and gave it a hard shove and heard it crash. A moment later she heard another crash and a Mycenean oath and knew he hadn't been able to stop in time to avoid the lamp and she'd gained a little time. She wove in and out of the portico, among outer and inner rooms, keeping in the shadows, hoping Kretheus had broken a leg or, better, his neck when he fell, but doubting it.

Her own spent breathing was so loud she couldn't hear anything else, and she shrank into the deepest shadow of a column to listen. He was coming but more slowly, cursing and, she thought, taking time to search the rooms that opened into the Court. She went on again, but not so fast, giving herself time to rest a little. She knew she couldn't keep up her original headlong running and she sensed that quiet movement was now more important than speed. As long as she made no sound and kept in the shadows she was safe. But in order to reach the hidden stairs she would have to come out into moonlight. She would have, from somewhere, to find strength for another, final spurt.

She leaned against the wall and hoped her heart would stop pounding. She'd lost the sound of pursuit again and she eased her head out from her shelter and quickly drew it in again. He was there, standing still in the moonlight, his head cocked for any sound, sniffing the air as if he were a boarhound and would track her by her scent.

There was nothing she could do except run for the stairs. He'd be bound to see her and follow, but she knew of a hiding place beside the wall and she'd have to chance it. She couldn't go back, if she would, because he barred her way. She gathered her flounced skirts about her, took a deep, hurting breath, and ran across the moon-gleaming white of the porch for the square of darkness that marked the opening to the stairs.

CHAPTER
NINETEEN

Thalamika, trying to breathe quietly, huddled behind a clump of low shrubs at the foot of the stairway outside the wall of the House of the Priest-King. She could see lights in all the tall houses that tumbled down the steep streets of Knossos and hear the hum of many voices of people keeping the feast of the Bull Games. She knew her hiding place was precarious. Kretheus was already on the stairs and, if he decided to search for her when he failed to see her on the moonlit path, he'd surely find her. But this bare refuge was her only chance, for she was spent and couldn't run another yard. She prayed he would think she'd rushed on to her aunt's house.

He was coming so quietly she couldn't follow his progress, but she knew he was there. She counted her heartbeats until she was sure he'd had time to pass her shelter, then lifted her head for a quick look. He was on the path going away from her and she thanked The Goddess for temporary deliverance, though she knew it was no more than that.

What should she do next? She couldn't leave while he was near, for the least movement would discover her to him. If he couldn't locate her in the next minute or two, would he go on to her aunt's house or would he come back searching the wayside? She couldn't do anything but wait and gather strength for another dash through the night if he started toward her. She relaxed a little with the decision, glad to wait quietly and breathe deeply and rest her aching legs.

She was aware as she lay on the warm ground of some change in the night. The moon still rode high and full through the field of stars. The lamps still glowed in the houses, and the sounds of lighthearted people still came clearly though distantly through the flower-scented air. But something had changed. Some quality of menace from the very earth which supported her seemed to communicate itself to her body, and she felt again the Goddess-sent tingling that warned her of danger.

She forgot Kretheus as her mind filled with awe and wonder. She stood up, the better to see the sky, snuffling the air. She felt, beneath her feet, a slight trembling as if the earth, too, were awe-filled. It lasted only a second and she thought she had imagined it. She turned around slowly, searching the four corners of the horizon, absorbed in an effort to bring her mind into harmony with The Goddess, to prepare herself to hear any message The Goddess might have for her.

A shout jerked her from absorption. Kretheus, returning, looking for her, had seen her clear in the moonlight. He began to run toward her.

She picked up her skirts and fled in the direction of the cypress grove, the nearest shadowed place where she might with good fortune lose herself in darkness. He called after her, "Wait, Thalamika! Wait! The Queen wants you."

Thalamika tried to run faster, but she could hear him coming closer, not calling now, saving his breath to outrun her. She couldn't get away from him. She hadn't rested enough, and she was besides oppressed with a feeling of suffocation that had nothing to do with lack of breath. The very night seemed to be holding her back. It wasn't any use. She'd just as well stop now, let him come up to her, let him kill her if he would. She thought despairingly of Andrios and wanted to cry out for their lost love but had no breath to do so. She turned with one last hope that she might be pulling ahead of her pursuer. He was, instead, much closer than she had expected, running along a path of light made by the moon.

She stopped and faced him and was aware again that the earth seemed to be moving. Seeing her waiting, he stopped running and came on slowly, his face set in bitter anger.

He was no more than ten paces from her when there was a sudden loud crack, as if the Lady of the Air had loosed her thunder, but at a distance. Kretheus stopped where he was, startled, and in that instant the earth began to shake and quiver and heave.

Thalamika pulled breath into her lungs. She understood the portents now. She knew why she had tingled with the Goddess-warning. Deep in his sea caves Poseidon, Earth-Shaker, was angry; was sending the earthquake to chasten the land-dwellers who had in some manner displeased him.

She had never before experienced earthquake but she had heard tales of it, for Knossos was often shaken, sometimes severely, sometimes only a little. She had no way of knowing which this would be, and her mind held no stored memory of how to protect herself. But instinct warned her to seek the high ground of the hills and gave new strength to her tired body. She ran over the heaving earth toward the hills and safety, hearing the high wail within the Palace and the crashing of stones thrown down by the Earth-Shaker's anger.

Above all other sounds, from close behind her, came a single cry so terrible it stopped her running. She looked over her shoulder to the place where Kretheus had been and saw clear under the moon that he was still standing there with a look of horror upon his face. And as she watched, unable to move, unable to turn away from that terrified expression in spite of the heaving earth, the ground itself split beneath his feet, split into a yawning hole, shivering the moonpath into a thousand shards of light. Kretheus, as if he had been a doll jerked from beneath, disappeared into the hole, and on the instant the earth heaved again and the split closed over him and the moonpath lay as before, calm and whole.

She stood open-mouthed, filled with awe, knowing that The God Himself had put forth his hand and wrought his own vengeance on the scoffer who would have profaned The Goddess and destroyed the land and the people of Crete. For the first time in her life she forgot her dread of Poseidon and lifted her arms toward the sea and raised the song of thanksgiving and praise to the Sea God.

As she finished the few words the earth trembled again, and again she knew fear for her own safety that set her feet in motion. She ran away from the Palace, not stopping until she came to the paved way beside the House of the Priestess. Her eyes noted that the small, beautiful palace was dark, but her mind made nothing of it, though at another time she would have wondered at this sign that the old High Priestess was away from her own place so late in the night.

She didn't slacken her pace until she had left the paved way and set her bare and aching feet upon the mountain path. Here, feeling in some measure safe, she stopped at last and sat upon a boulder and leaned her head forward until it rested on her knees. She stayed there for uncounted minutes, emotion-spent, too tired to wonder what had happened in Knossos and Amnisos; too tired to be glad she was alive; too tired to think about Andrios.

A soft *Who-o-o-,who-o-o-o* roused her and a small gray owl brushed her cheek with its wing and flew away, startled. She lifted her head then and looked toward the Palace stretching its length far below her. Even as she looked its lights flickered and seemed to sway and she shuddered, knowing the Earth-Shaker was busy again. But here in the hills the ground was steady, and she pushed herself to her feet and started to climb toward the cave.

She hadn't reached the bend in the path when she heard her name called searchingly, and tried to answer and couldn't make her voice heard. The next moment Andrios came running toward her. His kilts were grimed and torn. The welt on his cheek where Minos' ring had grazed him was open again and bleeding a little. His eyes were rimmed white with weariness and were just losing, at sight of her, a look of frantic worry. But she saw none of this as she sank upon the ground, knowing that there was no more need to struggle. He came to her and picked her up, kissing her hair and eyes and cheeks as if he must reassure himself that she was here with him. He said over and over, "Thalamika, Thalamika, Thalamika," as he carried her up the remainder of the path and into the cave.

He set her down on the cloak they had all used in the morning and leaned over her, still calling her name, until Chryses pushed him aside. "She'll do well enough, Lord Andrios," Chryses said. "She's only tired and hungry. Leave her to me and get water from the spring. And do you, Lady Philona, bring food."

Thalamika came slowly back to the world around her from some shadowed place where she'd been since Andrios had found her. She hadn't, she thought, lost consciousness, for she had felt the cool water Philona poured over her face and hands and bruised feet. She had drunk the cup Chryses held for her and eaten a barley-and-honey cake and some fruit. But she had known these things in a daze. Now she was aware of others; of Andrios patting her hand awkwardly, looking worried again; of Philona, pale and frightened with Drupos' arm around her; of Chryses, calm and efficient, making her mistress comfortable; and of another, shadowy figure outside the light thrown by the lamp hanging from an outcrop of rock. The shadow figure bothered her, and she peered into the gloom and said irritably, "Who's that in the shadows?"

The figure moved lightly, gracefully, toward her. "It's I, Lady Thalamika," Sarpedon said, and Thalamika stared at the bull mask reflecting the lamplight from his belt, and at the marks of tears still on his face.

"Sarpedon," she said wonderingly and gripped Andrios' arm and sat up, feeling a little dizzy. "What—why—?"

Her face puckered in bewilderment as she tried to

understand. There was something so comic in her look that, seeing it, the others found sudden release in laughter from pent-up tensions, and the cave echoed and re-echoed with the sound of mirth.

Thalamika shut her eyes to keep from spilling the tears building behind them. She was so tired, and they were all laughing at her and she didn't understand about Sarpedon. It had been a night of dread and who could say what might be happening in Knossos, and yet they were laughing.

"An—dri—os!"

The long-drawn call came from outside the cave and the laughter ceased and Thalamika opened her eyes and forgot her tears. Andrios went to the cave mouth and called, "Here, Spyros. Come up to us." He came back and sat beside Thalamika and pulled her head onto his shoulder, as if she'd been a tired child. "Spyros has been to Knossos looking for you, Thalamika. He'll tell us what has happened there."

Spyros came into the cave and looked at Thalamika and said testily, "Why didn't you come to the bastion, Thalamika? We've all been nearly frantic with worry over you."

Before she could answer Andrios said, "Let her rest now, Spyros. She's half-dead with exhaustion. She can tell us her story later." He shifted his arm a little so he could see her face. "There's just one thing now, Thalamika, if you can tell us. Kretheus."

Thalamika pulled away from him, remembering the long-drawn cry and the crack in the earth's crust where a path had been. "He—he was swallowed by the earth," she said so low they could hardly hear her. "The whole world was shaking and I was running and I heard a terrible cry and looked and saw the earth open beneath him and close again and he was trapped and . . ."

". . . punished by the anger of Poseidon!" Andrios said quickly, and Sarpedon added softly, "As my father said it would be."

Thalamika was suddenly shaking with the remembered horror of Kretheus' entombment. She started to speak again, but Andrios pulled her back against him and said, "Don't think about it, Thalamika. He deserved whatever evil came to him. Rest now, and listen to Spyros."

Spyros said, "The earth is still now in Knossos. The Palace and some houses were damaged a little but the harm's not great. The Nubians are guarding the embassy from Mycenae, but without their leader the others of the Myceneans are helpless and as simple as children. They keep protesting and demanding to be taken to Minos and to be told where Kretheus is. The Nubians pay no attention, and the Myceneans are wild!" He smiled a little, thinking of the frustration on the faces of the haughty ambassadors. "Nitos is safe enough in the pit, untouched by Poseidon's anger, but I left him there. I . . ." He paused and looked at Sarpedon before he went on. "I had word of the Queen. It is not good."

Sarpedon said, "Have no pity for my feelings, Spyros. The Queen is no longer dear to me. Tell us."

"She was, until we knew about Kretheus, supposed to be the only person counted dead in the shaking. When it began she ran from the hall of the feasting out into the Central Court, shrieking curses on Thalamika of Phaistos and calling for Kretheus. As she went beneath the Sanctuary of the Bloodless Sacrifice, one of the Horns of Consecration toppled from its place and fell upon her and crushed her."

"Now is my father's death avenged by the Bull-Tamer," Sarpedon said.

"Minos dead!" Even saying the words gave them no real meaning to Thalamika. Minos couldn't be dead. He was their High Priest and King.

Andrios told her then what had happened at the Inner Sanctuary, and she got up and went to the Young King, knowing now why he wore the mask at his belt, and knelt before him and touched the mask and the seal of kingship which he held out to her. He stood tall while she, as Priestess of the Great Goddess, acknowledged his power as Priest and King, but when she had done he gave her his hand and raised her to her feet and said in a small, shaky voice, "I'm still Sarpedon, Lady Thalamika, and I've—I've so much to learn." He sounded lost and forlorn, and she forgot he was Priest-King of Crete and thought only of the boy who had lost both his father and mother in a single night and put her arms around him to comfort him.

Spyros broke the spell that held them all. "What of the Mycenean fleet, Andrios, and the port and the merchants?"

"The merchants are well guarded in their houses and Amnisos is quiet. Tomorrow . . ."

Philona spoke then for the first time, and her voice was low and fierce. "What of my—what of Phelleus the Merchant? What will happen to him?"

"What the Priest-King wills," Andrios said and looked at Sarpedon.

The Young King spoke slowly as if he were trying to

think through, for the first time, the problem of judgment. "All the merchants will have to be punished somehow. I think—I think it would be best to banish the leaders—like your father, Philona, though I'm sorry to say it, for you have helped save us all."

Philona said, "He deserves worse for his treachery. But I'm glad he'll just be banished. Though I hate him, he is still my father."

"The rest of the merchants," Sarpedon went on, "will be, I think, fined a little and warned against future treachery. I expect they just got carried away with the idea of running our trade and will be glad enough to behave when they've had time to think it over. Is—is that all right, Andrios?"

"Yes," Andrios said, proud that Sarpedon in his first decision as King had shown good sense and mercy in his judgment. "I'm sure, once the leaders are away, the others won't trouble us again, especially since the Mycenean fleet is destroyed. The sailors are in bonds and the ships will be converted to the use of our own merchants. Our fleet went out to seek them as soon as I sent word to our Captain that King Lyssus' war fleet was almost certainly hiding near Amnisos. They were lurking behind the island of Dia. They weren't expecting us. The sailors were playing at draughts or lounging on the decks. One of them explained to our Captain they'd been told no one would be on the alert for them, for everyone would be at the feast. The officers were eating and drinking under the deck awnings. They hadn't even set a watch. Our ships came on them suddenly. They had no time to get their arms and they surrendered at once. Now, if we could only be sure Poseidon's anger is finished . . ."

Chryses said, "How many times did the earth heave, O Mistress?"

Thalamika stirred and said, "No longer your mistress, Chryses, but your friend, for you are free from this time, as I promised." She saw the tears on Chryses' face and went on quickly to answer her question. "There were three heavings, Chryses. Three separate times the earth moved, and each time the shaking lasted for the space of three breaths."

Chryses, ignoring the tears of happiness, nodded. "It is well, then," she said. "It is according to the pattern and the end of it has come."

Thalamika said curiously, "How can you be sure?" and Chryses answered, "I have known many such quakings in the country of my people. I recognize the signs. The quakes come in threes. If there were to be another three besides, we should have known it by now, for the time for repeating is past."

Andrios said, "Poseidon's wrath was not for us this time but for our enemies. Praised be the name of the Earth-Shaker," and Thalamika walked to the opening of the cave and drew in deep breaths of the cool night air. Below her, lights showed in Knossos, burning steadily, and further along she could just make out in the moonlight the line of the sea and the port of Amnisos. There was no disorder in the feel of the night now, no tingling within herself to show that The Goddess was sending warning. The weeks of uncertainty were over and only new Priest-King would remind them of the death of Minos. Her eyes smarted with tears for him, but she knew that even young Sarpedon would grow in time to miss him less and less until memory was gentled and no longer painful.

She turned and came back to the group seated on the cave floor and told them the story of her evening. When she had finished Andrios got up from the floor and lifted his arms and said in a voice full of rejoicing, "Crete is safe and Minos is revenged. The God Himself has destroyed those who would destroy us. All glory and praise to the Earth-Shaker and to the Great Goddess, Earth Mother, Lady of Crete."

As the last word dropped between them, Spyros took his double-pipes from his kilts and blew the first notes of the paean of thanksgiving. Sarpedon's clear, sweet voice took up the song and the rest of them, one by one; Andrios the Cupbearer, Drupos the Boxer, the Lady Thalamika and the Lady Philona, and Chryses who had been a slave and now was free, joined the song.

When the paean was done Andrios took Thalamika's hand and said, "Come then. It's time to cry the new Priest-King in the Palace and the streets of Knossos and to send runners through all the land of Crete to tell his name. Let us go home and begin the new reign in mercy and peace under Sarpedon, Priest-King of Crete."

Sarpedon looked at Andrios and smiled and stepped ahead of his friend and counselor to the mouth of the cave. He lifted the bull mask and set it upon his head and motioned to the Nubians who waited outside. Moonlight fell softly upon the amethyst and gold of the Priest-King's sealstone, and they all saw clearly the Labrys and Horns of Consecration of the royal line incised in the stone. Thalamika whispered to Andrios, "He'll make a good Priest-King—with your help, my Andrios," and

Andrios said, "May it please Poseidon and The Goddess to make him so," and brought her hand into the curve of his arm as they followed the boy, proud and lonely in his kingship, but still moving as if he were a winged creature, down the mountain to the House of the Priest-King.